LEVITATION

Hey Ben,

This book might
be terrible but the cover
is great. Hope you like it
anyway /xxx
Ruthlestun

Other books by Laynie Browne

Gravity's Mirror (Primitive Editions, 2000)

The Agency of Wind (AVEC, 1999)

Clepsydra (Insress, 1999)

L O R E (Instress, 1998)

Rebecca Letters (Kelsey Street Press, 1997)

One Constellation (Leave Books, 1994)

Hereditary Zones (Boog Literature, 1993)

ACTS

OF

LEVITATION

Laynie Browne

Spuyten Duyvil
PO Box 1852
Cathedral Station
NYC 10025
http://spuytenduyvil.net
1-800-886-5304

The author wishes to thank the editors of the following publi-
cations, where excerpts from this book initially appeared:
A.BACUS, Duration: A Journal of International Writing, Key
Satchel, The Poetry Project Web Site, Scout, and Vox Populi:
1999 Seattle Poetry Festival Anthology.

Grateful thanks to the following individuals for their generous
readings of this work: Leonard Brink, Brad Davidson, Sarah
Getz, Jeanne Hueving, Lisa Jarnot and Lissa Wolsak. Thanks to
Dennis Willows and Billie Swalla for providing housing at
Friday Harbor Laboratories and Roscoff Marine Station, where
much of this work was written.

Library of Congress Cataloging-in-Publication Data

Browne, Laynie, 1966-
    Acts of Levitation/Laynie Browne.
        p.cm.
    ISBN 1-881471-94-2
    1. Creation (Literary, artistic, etc.)--Fiction. 2. Photography-
-Fiction. 3. Women--Fiction. I. Title.

PS3552.R748 A63 2002
813'.54--dc21   2002067006

for Lee Ann Brown

ACTS OF LEVITATION

PART ONE:
Amelia-Clare

PART TWO:
The Corridor

Part Three:
Book of Gossamer and Light

One can own a mirror
does one then own the reflections
that may be seen in it?
—Veronica Forrest-Thomson
"Zettel"

Part One:

Amelia-Clare

AMELIA ENTERS THE ROOM, OR ENTER AMELIA, OR THE SIMPLE ACT OF ENTERING A ROOM

*f*rom Clara's notebook, misplaced October (year?)

> A waterbird did gingerly
> in several steps each lifted   (sound) (lake)
>
> whose reflection held in ripples.
> Still a dark spot, silhouetted
> Long agile neck she glided into the room,
> Bill supposed, neck collapsed.

The thousand and one dimes on the surface of the waters (sound) (lake).

She glided into the room with her reflection diagonally in front of her, parting the carpet with partridges and orchestra.

He raised his arms and the trumpets began, the water bird began, the trill began.

She glided into the room, partial to the floating rib, with a purse full of blood, a handful of matches.

She glided into the room more or less elegant as a water moccasin, an occasion.

She carried herself as a carriage more or less precarious to the tides. The room was full of woodpeckers, or the sounds of heads knocking against wood.

I have to warn you, she said, they are not exactly identical. The tables were deeply congregated, set within a sea of partial humming.

Sidewise, she glanced into the room.

The room upon wheels.
Her feet slightly lifted the air below them.

She tranced into the room. She had once supposed herself to be eloquent. To stroll into a room. But the room was merely parted.

The language at the deeply concentrated tables was rising up from lips, a visible smoke.

She rose and perhaps beheld the head of a pirate, or a spider at the other end of the room. This gave her a destination.

She preened her plumage, and proceeded ahead.

"Where" is a construct of watery minds.

The waterbird gingerly disappeared.

A CHORUS OF DIMLY CONCENTRATED TABLES

As she lifted her summer brow, her heels now slightly grazing the floor, the concentrated tables dimmed. The heads gathered. Moment clasped. Arms around backs around chairs. Faces lifted like lilies. She had vanished into the hive. And now could no longer glide, as her circular wheels entrapped within each square of honeycomb. Backs around arms around clasps. Clatter and chiffon demise. Scalloped-Neck perforce chattered, with Sundered-Lip, gathering spectators, perceiving, without half looking up, the newly arrived "girl." For though she was no longer a "girl" she was perceived as such, and therefore may as well have been. She heard her name murmured among corners. Faint introductions commenced. And then everyone was seated, and everything began. The performer entered, adjusted a microphone, drew the eyes of the chorus in upon himself using tiny golden threads. Amelia quickly upon the heels of the early departing, rose, made a farewell toss to anyone, possibly no one, and left.

The woman, Amelia, evaporated down a narrow cobblestoned block, beyond alleys and dumpsters in the quickly spreading dusk. Her hands as maps out before her. The "girl" regarded, however remained, and was discussed in tones far less faint than those which had been taken with introductions. Scalloped-Neck rose now not half but fully flushed. The tables were no longer dim. Perhaps some had noticed her skimming effect, as if the floor had been covered by several inches of water. Others perplexed noticed her brimming. She had in fact tried to prevent the gliding, would have wished to have been perceived as merely walking into the room. The simple act of entering a room, even this remained suspect, so how at the outset could she be seen? All of this mire escaping from the lips of the concentrated tables while Amelia had been blown down so many dusty streets. As she approached her small room she could already smell the sleep upon her sheets.

SHE GRACES THE CEILING

The first time it occurred she was seen kneeling as a child. Kneeling for what reason? Her mother supposed her to be devout.

But there was no religion in the house. She walked into the room to find her daughter kneeling several feet above the floor. Her head tucked into her chest as a swan's.

THIS BODY OR NAME

Amelia—with knowledge of one block, and one friend who would certainly desert her. But that was just as well. Inside the quietness of her bedside candle amidst boxes and shadows she had arrived.

She returned to the apartment which had meant waiting in line, or luck with applications. She took the floorthrough before she had seen it, as the rules required, since after all it looked over the park. Not having noticed much of anything but the moon from the window of October over heavy leaves of the streetlamp. To locate the sky was some accomplishment.

She placed the bed against one wall and watched it roll, or rather fly across the room. The slope, she hadn't noticed upon examining the place downstairs. Pens rolled off of her desk. Plates slid from her table. The kitchen she supposed once used to be a closet. A mouse lived in the stove, who after her meals would jump among the burners. It was the top floor, and there was no fire escape. But the roof was plausible. The radiators spoke. The six flights didn't tire her unless she were to carry anything besides her body.

She contained within her palms the fleeting nature of fluidity. This was also known as youth. Submerged below a less than shallow gloss. The gloss is the water under which she can breathe. It appears to be shallow, but there is no shallowness involved. For any person who can breathe underwater is often seen as a witch. In looking over her history, it remained unclear how she had crossed many overtures of water. It became unclear at times what exactly she had held in her palms. There was no perfection in her tale, except that in looking over her history, unless one had been her exactly, it could never be seen how it was that she had managed to pull herself through what appeared to be a series of charmed obstacles.

Night has swallowed her, pressed in along the linings of the day, caused her to refract. She will swallow her tongue. This which intoxicates, to remain unpossessed. Unafraid in the way a child is unafraid.

This person or form, she told herself, this body or name, is less dear than the one expression of the many, the comprehensible swallowing of the rose.

The labyrinth remains within, and this city one bridge to that. This wandering within a curve of beginning which never ends. Or never weeping upon a pencil's tapered edge. As if a pencil could hold sway more than suggestion.

THE CHORUS SPECULATES FAR LESS FAINTLY

"The curve of her aubergine gown, or was it russet, yes russet with golden peacock feathers full, or ripe grain spilling, and a beast upon the stone ground. "
"That was a fabulous charade."
"The canopies of their triangular hats, the golden trim. These issues of falling stars."
The program had ended. The conversation was rising up from lips, a visible smoke. The dimly lit tables couched together as if to form a type of syntax.
"The girl?"

"When did she arrive, and where from?"

"The truth about her parentage: She was an orphan." Scalloped-Neck interrupts. "A tornado knocked over the graves so that when she arrived, her mother's tombstone was broken into indecipherable rubble."

"Indecipherable?"

"Indecipherable."

"And she found nothing further of her?"

"Rubble only."

"And her father?"

"Her father was Baron Redwing Von- some one or other, you must recall—"

"Yes, born 1895. He was a wildlife conservationist. He 'loved nature throughout his life.' "

Terrible laughter.

Sundered-Lip arises, "What is this chittering? She said so herself, his tombstone reads, 'he loved nature.'"

"And his fate?"

"He was the first known Westerner to have been eaten by a Komodo dragon."

"Now that, was a fabulous charade."

Angrily, "This is no charade!"

"No stories from local pearl divers." Dark-Eye-In-Lashes submits, "told above or below water?"

High-Forehead wanders, "neither, but the truth from the girl herself. Komodo island, Indonesia, Indian Ocean. Komodo dragon = Varanus Komodoenis. Van Steyn in 1912, Dutch military officer collected the first specimen. Twenty wickedly splayed griffinlike talons, backward slanting teeth, like a shark, amphibious and carnivorous. With poisonous saliva. Eleven feet long, over 500 pounds."

"The island was craggy and dramatic. Sandalwood horses."

"All that was found of him were his hat, camera, and a bloody shoe."

"Still I submit, a fabulous charade. A mother of rubble, and a father destroyed by a beast. Was the girl raised by wolves? And how did she stumble into these parts? What is her business here?"

AMELIA BLOTS HER LIPS, AT NIGHT, ON A BALCONY

And so to dawn a time, a gown, no less obvious minister would marry the present to the past. Or an orchestrating temperature, if only she had known where or when exactly to listen. The music is the ultimate thermometer of any setting. And yet music also contains color, momentum, physicality, as an animal taking place, yet a different animal, or element, or narrative each decibel, note, or sinister movement. Whose adagios. Whose sound of very sound.

She mustn't compare herself to the present, to odd visitors, to the known. They want her to be "something namable" "Something repeatable." She will not desist. The music then slows and she approaches a balcony. The night darkens, though it was already dark. Or perhaps she blots her lips. The impression of which had a marked effect upon the music, which at the moment did not desist, nor did it blot. She approaches a balcony filled with her once accomplishments, or adagios, yet the balcony also contains color, "something repeatable" which she is not. She wanders nearly far or greatly darkening her eyes whose reciprocity approach "something namable", though she will not name this.

Though this will not be named, nor will it perch. No meaningful canary has wandered from her lips. As if to say hello. Each sound then a small silver hatchet, with which one might defeat the structure of the balcony entirely. But she must look down into the orchestra. She must view this "something namable" which she is not, this "sinister movement", the moment unblotted, moving or perhaps blustering towards her, though no thermometer could counter the present darkness which had simply grown darker in the sense that she had approached it more fully. If this balcony were to surrender and to grow brighter at her approach, then she might simply lie down and remove her many attachments, those which allow her to wander, those which allow her to be still, those which allow her to blot the color of the repeatable darkening which surrounds her quite predictably, but for which she was not quite ever prepared. This was perhaps her most romantic accomplishment. She did not accept blindly the duality of night and day. The duality of colors pressed against their own metaphors.

Reciprocity approaches a boat and fills mountains with light. The mountains rise from their slumber and inhale. For this she is never quite prepared. The adagio which follows is constructed solely of darkness.

CLARA OF THE EMERALD BOTTLE

The emerald bottle supposes. The bottle which spoke to Clara, as if Clara were the only one present. Her eye took many photographs of the light that late afternoon, lilting through glass, the green bottle in line of light from the window, frosted. Her corresponding green eye lit. Nobody noticed this, as her concentrated gazes would often "listen" to an object while one spoke to her. Hands in lap or tracing a circular pattern upon a table top, around a wineglass. Her eyes listening and also pardoned.

Her eye, the emerald bottle. The truth was her corresponding eye was duly bored. Banter could be spoken through, or heard through her dimensionless sky. She began to pick up upon what was said of her, how she was excused from a particular type of social engagement, and began to use these others' descriptions of herself as additional screens. When she did not want to answer to the idiocy of mundane questioning she would fail to reply. If her reputation preceded her into any room, so did her survivalist tactics. And holding out her hand to any charmed subject, no one suspected beneath her mirroring, what she was protecting or effacing. The public smile grew at times weary, but did not thin or weaken. She had been trained for this type of public display. She was in the middle of such a congregation when first seeing Amelia. Quietly waltzing with herself in a corner. She had hidden the gliding for once successfully, and walked ever so securely upon the ground. But was that merely another trick? Amelia saw her, pivoted her lip. Looked down once again. Here was an expert. Within these realms to be explored everything is partial, if only one were to have a benevolent escort. One who at least can claim a map.

Was she serenely waltzing? This is what Clara called it, a type of interior rocking, almost undetectable. A few cradling steps upon the lenient wood beneath.

CLARA

She had been alone, and the silence commenced to speak to her. A form emerged from patterns of dust. Rising, a slip of sunlight. A streamer of muslin strewn across her window. A shadow inhabits a dress pinned to her wall. She at once recognizes the figure. The tilt of her head, falling against her angular chin. In the dust she has been silenced, commences to speak with sunlight, the tilt of a young window. The arch companion of a dress. The sunlight condenses the figure, a streamer of form slipping from beginnings.

In the sunlight she has recognized the shadow guest. The angular speech of dust. She had once been alone, and now she has been rhymed. She sits in the windowsill, chin dropped to her chest. Hands out before her, testing the light.

Now that she has appeared, she needs only finishing. In red ink, upon a bedsheet. She reaches for a pendant and douses over a glass of tired water. Shall she remain? For how many revolutions? She counts the pennies beside. And the hexagram which follows?

She reads:

"The yielding comes from and gives form to the firm, the firm ascends and gives form to the yielding. Things should not unite abruptly and ruthlessly. Grace is the same as adornment."

Pleated as a penny which needed finishing.

"The most perfect grace consists not in external ornamentation but in allowing the original material to stand forth, beautified by being given form."

A new form is tenderly hung.

"The judgment: Success in small matters. It is favorable to undertake something. It is favorable to bestow an aspiring form with light, clear and still. If the form is contemplated, the changes of time can be discovered."

If the forms of humans are contemplated, one can shape the word. Note: The text of the commentary does not appear to be intact. There seems to be a sentence missing before, 'this is the form of a dress pinned to a wall.' An explanation of the foregoing sentence would follow. But something of the sort must in fact be presupposed. The firm and yielding unite alternately and construct forms: this is the form of the dress."

She looks up blinking, from the window to the dress, to the text in front of her, all of which have become inter-mingled.

In the first case it is the line that bestows form directly and therefore brings about sheen, whereas the ascending hem, by lending content, the principle of the form is frilled. The otherwise empty window can work itself out. It is favorable for 'the small' to undertake something." The penny is small. A person or window.

"The image. Blue smoke at the foot of the stairs. The inverse of the preceding afternoon."

It was a theoretical, not a practical turn of mind which had caused her to pin the dress to the wall, and then to imagine one who might wear it.

"The one above attains her will.   Note, it is a ten-dency throughout to counteract overemphasis of form by means of content. A strong nature forgoes all ornament. She chooses plain white. "

INVERSE OF THE PRECEDING AFTERNOON

She sat in a corner, and she, the other sauntered in, saw her, and sat at her table. Which she was sitting and which sauntering? But who is known to saunter and who is safer sitting, quietly swung into a corner table, with chairs whose delicate legs will not collapse beneath? The meeting was accidental, but was bound to occur on such an Autumnal day, where refreshment of one's senses is required. She smiled, and she smiled as well. And this is where the afternoon begins. Because Amelia had been looking for just such a twin, one who claimed to know her way somewhat amidst the labyrinth. And Clara, had been looking for just such a twin, one who was furthermore lost, but did not mind so much as there was someplace to be found. Amelia's path was strewn with the tired blossoms thrown by Clara's onlookers. Although some had been crushed, their fragrances remained sweet. Clara was in need of the youthful companionship of one who barely trod upon the ground. It was as if she had divined this companion. As if the dress had fallen from its place among the treasures pinned upon her walls, and been filled with the curious shadow of form which sat across from her now. She at once recognized the figure. The tilt of her head, the unornamented expression falling across her face.

A Song Which Sleeps Inside A Box

The shop gave the impression of being crowded, even when no one was within it. Behind the counter sat a woman with an owl like face, her chin propped upon decorated hands. They stumbled down the unkempt aisles. Giddy with the sudden gust of warmth and pulling off their gloves to better touch the old volumes and cutlery, fallen bridles, dented kettles, glass jewels behind counters of glass, precarious bicycles, alabaster grapes, a crepe covered pram, a box of screw-on skates, piles of old photographs. As they proceeded through the sinewy walkways, they adorned themselves with artifacts. A tophat. A sailor's coat. A smoking jacket. Ears beginning to tingle, toes beginning to sting, slowly remembered. Amelia fell heavily into a rocker and began sorting through a basket of old clock mechanisms. Clara was standing over a sideboard, opening and closing the lid to a music box. The instrument could be seen by lifting a small worn velvet panel inside. The toothed barrel operating on the vibrating tongues. She wound the little latch on its side, and held it open finally, listening. The song was unfamiliar. Sand being dropped slowly. Clara approached in a felt hat with spidery veil pulled down to her chin. She placed the music box in Amelia's hands. White porcelain lid, a painted rose in the center, bronze legs curled into the shape of swans. Underneath was an inscription:

For Amelina, a song which sleeps inside this box until needed.

AMELIA AND CLARA (AT THE BEACH, AN INTERLUDE)

Looking out the window of the train, fog moving in thickets. Strains, appearing and disappearing.
"An hour is a luxurious pendulum which swings."
"Cressy."
"Is that what you see along the streambed?"
"Crestfallen acres."
"Pertaining to twilight."
"A cricket then?"

"I who know how to be in the country."

"You, who know how to be in the country?"

"Yes, *Lily of the lawn.*"

"I imagined you might have preferred a dictionary."

"Three or four large dictionaries filled with magnificent words which no one ever uses."

"And where might these words reside then, beyond the book which guards them?"

"Naturally, the words reside in the house."

"Along with red-winged blackbirds?"

"And an exhausted appendix—out painting sparrows."

They turn from the window, still covered in dampness. Sun breaking through in patches. The train pauses, resumes its flight. They begin once again.

"If I were to board a train and you were to board a train, how much faster would the octopus be able to open the jar containing the hermit crab?"

"Where did the octopus get its violet cape?"

"The sea demands a fitting costume."

"I have heard—"

"What is sound if not second to light?"

"Are you certain of the distance in that equation?"

"As certain that there are artists who carry light, and those who carry sound, and those with capital letters only."

Clara considers, "I am a polite archer with my camera, but this says nothing about my "aim" which is often prior to the vision being stabbed."

"And aiming "at" is the emphasis which insists upon itself more fluently than any marker."

"If I were to board a train, I am also a marker because speed has no image, and if there were a ray of disentangled seeing—"

"Disentanglement has everything to do with the octopus, nothing to do with sight."

"If I were to board a spoon—"

"Very likely."

"If I were to board a spoon, I would travel at the same rate as the child who has placed her head down upon her desk in the middle of the afternoon."

The train again pauses. They step out into a vast expanse of light which meets the water several bounds off.

"Yes, the afternoon is childish."

"I wish you wouldn't insist on the photons traveling beside us. I speak less fluently in light, more often conversing in spoons."

"I see."

"See the afternoon?"

They hear a child in the distance. Small steps approaching.

"With golden curls, he must be insisting to go down there, where the water meets its reflection."

"The golden head will insist, upon which the blue dragon-fly."

"Consider that the madrona must enter into her vision, the kelp forest. "

"The thousand and one commas along the water."

They bend their heads together, like pilgrims, sitting upon a picnic table, shoulders sloped.

They imagine the child only heard in the distance, blond and grinning. The sound of thighs clapping together. The child then is in front of them.

"Dustin," the child asks an invisible companion, "do you like my new pet?" (Holding a large stipe of bull kelp).

"What is that?" a voice replies. The child runs past them carrying a pail of water towards a more conscious pail of sand.

CONSTRUCTIONS GALLERY

They wander. Glancing about them. Light flowing into their eyes. Eyes casting light onto the immaculate blond floors of the gallery.

They move through a series of habitations. First, a collection of microscopic fish larvae projected along the sides of a dark winding corridor. Water trickling down the walls. Mild wafting overhead. The projections appear for several seconds, and are replaced, as if a page has been turned. Or so it seems to Amelia. She looks up, a shadow in the semi-dark.

"I can't quite see." Clara frowns.

"This has nothing to do with sight. I'm lost between—" the sounds have drowned her speech.

"Between? Sight has everything to do with entanglement." Her face covered with flitting images as she leans closer to the wall.

"Between the pages," she pauses, "of this watery book."

"The pages of a book?" She has not seen them until now. They cross over her hands, decorating her palms with yellow light. "What sort of book?" she continues.

"The sort that keeps turning," though once the words escape her she isn't sure why she has chosen them. "A projection at least."

Clara reflects, "Books collapse history. They collapse when you touch them." The images seem to be crawling now, across her face. "It contains no story I hope" she adds, running her hands along the wet walls.

"It does collapse." Amelia answers, standing very close to the wall, gazing at pink cylindrical larvae, rippling with cilia. She hadn't found the word before now. She had thought of erosion, a slower falling.

"I would expect," Clara returns, "that it would." The projections slide away and their skins are restored as they emerge from the dark corridor. Blinking in the full light. "Then you've already succeeded" Clara adds.

"Succeeded?" She muses impossibly over "success" which seems unlikely, impossible, certainly premature.

Clara smiles, but Amelia cannot see this. "Don't suppose that I haven't already guessed. You've shown me nothing, but I have guessed."

She feels the color rising up her neck, so many fingers upon her cheek. They seem not to be her own.

Clara's air of always knowing, always guessing. Even though she has not a clue as to what might have possibly been guessed she feels suddenly exposed. "What have you guessed?" She returns pointedly.

"I've guessed that you may be making observations." She twirls her hand in the air, an ornamental flourish, a somewhat mocking finish.

Amelia has said nothing so telling as to reveal herself. She doesn't wish to speak. Only to listen to one who seems to say everything before it is spoken. Her gaze arranges things. Everything comes to pass as she chooses.

She follows the vague thread which has been dropped to another landing where projections turn and collapse once again, and thinks the movement of her thought is similar to this. Verbal sight.

Clara expects some reply. She continues, "is my encouragement lost?"

Amelia needs no further prodding, but still she hesitates. How to describe an occupation so much within that it barely may rest audibly upon a page? She did wish to be heard though, and so she began "—I am inventing the memories of a young girl who identifies herself with objects to such an extent that she finds any movement of them intolerable—." She pauses here, though this does not seem enough.

"What will occur if the objects are moved?" Clara asks, her face expectant.

"The light will not glint as much—across the face of her bureau. The grains and markings will fail to articulate particular expressions which she has begun to rely upon." She waits for a reply before continuing her thought, for Clara to add something. But Clara is quiet at least outwardly. They step out of the wet corridor and approach the next exhibit where they remove their stockings and shoes, and enter tunnels of soft green felt, through which they crawl, bare-legged.

"Like the chair which I always supposed to be scowling? The secret lives of furniture?" Clara asks, after what seems a great distance. Amelia turns back into the tunnel and sees her green shadow. She has been met. "Mere projections?"

"Yes, one image replaces another. At least you could argue that she sees what she wishes to see." The tunnel grows thinner for several feet, veers sharply to the left, then seems to expand to its original width.

"And she wishes to see?"

Amelia does not answer quickly. What does she wish to see? What is she seeing now? The green tunnel envelops them, contains the illusion that they need never emerge. She studies the artificial light. Is comforted by the sense of enclosure. She repeats the question, silently, and then ventures, "She wishes only to have found an opening. Bred by familiarity." And then she asks herself again as they reach the other end of the tunnel and sit replacing their socks and shoes. She asks herself what she wishes to see, and how it is that she wishes to see as Clara sees. A bit lost and a bit giddy in her wake. As they stand to leave a man is emerging from the tunnel in shorts. He looks at them awkwardly for a moment until

33

they vacate the bench. They descend a spiral staircase to reach the next interior. Their shoes click on metal steps. It seems, she thinks holding her arms, that the temperature drops as they descend.

Amelia continues, "One day a mirror which she has earlier ignored, is placed in a position so that she cannot avoid her own reflection."

"How does she respond?"

Amelia had here hoped for a suggestion. She turns her inflection toward her companion. "How does she respond?" She smiles. She places her sad heroine in front of the mirror. She stands there and loses all sense of herself. She considers. At the bottom of the stairs they find themselves within a stone sanctuary below the ground. Blue and white marbles continually roll up the slate walls, and disappear.

Finally Clara offers vaguely, "She has no option certainly," as if to solve the question.

Amelia agrees, "Yes. That's all that occurs. She dissolves there, in terms of surfaces." The marbles make a gravel-like sound as they course up the steep walls. In the center of the room is a pile of ashes. As if to solve the question. Dampness. She holds her arms again. She can smell the water in the air.

"The work collapses?"

"The bulk of the writing will be there, in the corridor." She grasps the railing and turns. "The girl looking into the mirror, realizing she is no longer an object."

"And the chair no longer scowls?"

"No longer." Clara looks displeased at this.

"The objects cease to speak to her? Appalling. How will she continue?"

"It is not certain whether or not she will take her reflection back." She sees now Clara's expression pale or pressing. Firm and distraught.

Clara looks unsure but says nothing. Her gestures speak persuasively. "Consider the problem. How long must she wait?"

"An entire, childish afternoon." She thinks an afternoon can seem as long. As long so as to be unbearable, mistaken for indefinite. The space seems suddenly small and cold. "She must wait. She must." She will not be lenient with this girl, plagued as she is by her own reflection.

They ascend from the chamber slowly, the last several steps in unison, and enter a dimly lit room where they take seats in folding chairs along one wall. A large placard reads:

Complete silence required while viewing
A Concert of Burning Paper.

The video shows a middle-aged man squatting, an unbound manuscript on his knee, feeding one page at a time into a bonfire. They remain for the duration of the loop, seven minutes, and then stand with the others to depart. Once they have cleared the silent room, Clara continues.

"I'm certain that she will take it back."

Amelia has forgotten to what she refers. She questions with her gaze.

"The girl will take her reflection back. A dangerous object—that mirror. What does it look like?"

Amelia considers, pretending to invent its dimensions, though she has already decided. "Like the mirror which hangs in your studio."

Clara's expression is doubtful. "On a clear day? Its clouds are misleading."

"Clouds?"

"Yes. You haven't noticed?" She looks concerned.

She nods. She has not.

"They appear like black lakes. Darkness."

"And they change—?"

"As the weather."

They stand now in front of a cryptic gallery map. Amelia still slightly disoriented. Then quickly—.

"I know the way back." They step over the threshold of an installation. The room is nearly dark. Elaborate chandeliers made from feline skeletons, dimly lit through tiger-eye painted shades, hang above a room covered in exquisite carpets. Holograms of panthers move silently throughout.

They walk among the holograms, at times through them. The panthers moving at various speeds. Stalking or leaping. They linger in this room at first separately, and then side by side. Shoulder to shoulder. Arms intertwined.

"There is great difficulty walking into the life of an object." Clara whispers. Her expression disguised by light.

Amelia considers, not knowing at all what she has in mind, not wanting to appear dim. " I can only imagine." Her expression lilts unknowingly.

"You don't realize then—" Clara returns the gaze but there is something in it she does not recognize. A sharpness which eludes her.

"Realize what?" She tightens her features, prepared. She dislikes this habit of Clara's, leading her along a path which seems already prepared for her distaste. All present in her expression—the doubt, the concentration, the confidence she lacks.

"It's already occurred." Clara answers, and as she does so she lowers her gaze and walks on, disengaging her arm in one fluid gesture. Amelia stands, very still within a crouching panther, uncertain of Clara's meaning. After a moment she reluctantly follows, and as she does so the panther begins to walk as if to follow her. It's already occurred, she repeats to herself as she steps out of the room. She acknowledges to herself as she does so that she seems still to walk within a hologram. She does not step out of the question. Or the question follows her as did the panther.

She blinks, since she finds herself suddenly in a sun-drenched space, where a book of six by eight feet is open upon a bed of combed sand on the floor. The plate reads:

Pages are of magnolia leaves pressed and pieced together,
bound with resin and twine, inscribed in an original encoded script
with pomegranate juice and hedgehog spines.

They stand before the book, marveling at the detail.
"You don't see? Already you have trespassed."

Amelia does not answer for a moment. She pauses,
"though you speak as if I were not—."

"As if you were not fluent—?"

"Fluent?" She echoes, questioning what has been
hidden.

"In the lives of objects." Clara makes this reply as if
her thoughts were apparent.

"Trespassing ?" Amelia is piecing together pieces of a
mosaic. Attempting to gather speech together into a clear
line of recognizable thought.

She turns her head with emphasis. "Precautions are
necessary."

"Precautions?" She asks again wondering, may I do
nothing but to repeat? Repetitions of crestfallen acres.
She senses hidden laughter. Is she being led? The words
reside inside the house. What house? She pictures herself
in the place of her heroine, standing, lily of the lawn, in
front of the studio mirror.

Clara continues, "Yes. To begin, what will your book
be constructed of?"

"My book. Though isn't it ours?" she pauses,
thinking, we have not gotten to that. Still out painting
sparrows

"Yes," Clara assents, "it will be ours." She smiles, "A collaboration."

"But how will the materials serve as precautions?" Amelia asks musing, the materials then, must be as significant as what they will contain. They demand a fitting costume.

"What we might use—" Clara pauses, "Gossamer?" she asks.

"Gossamer pages?" And she suddenly is able to lapse. And where might these words reside beyond the book which guards them? This is not verbal sight, she tells herself. She enters the interior, suspending all doubt. "Light? I speak less fluently in light." She begins to unfold. "Gossamer pages—."

"Inscribed with light." The room is filled. The image hangs in front of them. They stand looking at each other. Now it has been determined, and then they look down again, to the book in front of them on the sand.

Amelia begins, "If it can only be read—in certain light, and. ..the thousand-and-one commas on the surface of the water."

"Can only be read—" Clara crosses her arms and walks across the room.

"At certain times—" Amelia adds nodding.

"And by certain inhabitants of the book." They pause here to reflect. The train pauses again.

"Naturally, the words will reside in the book, and might not be visible from the outside."

Amelia wonders, for one inside there can be no outside. The outside is the object only, and the inside is the contemplation of that. She goes on aloud. "It can only be read under certain conditions, by those who have trespassed. By those who travel by placing their heads down in the middle of the afternoon."

"By those who know how to dwell within a book." Clara says stepping in close again.

Amelia acknowledges there will be those who turn away, who find nothing, and chooses this.

They step away and pass briefly through a small partitioned room painted black. A projection of a large cauldron is in the center, actual smoke pouring out. Scent of dragon's blood, faintly. There is a larger room up ahead, but first they pass a glass door leading into a courtyard. They step out and proceed down a stone pathway into an intricate true-to-scale garden formed entirely from various metals, stones and glass.

Clara kneels to smell a cluster of what appear to be red crystal-blossoms. "If I were to pluck this bergamot, would it continue to flower?" Her face against the glossy, faceted whorls.

"In some form certainly." I who know how to be in the country. She fingers the stiff leafy bracts. Somewhat fragile leaflets tinged with red. Clara stands. She turns again, her face distinct now from the others below. Amelia reaches a bed of glass-lavender, caressing the stalks. They pass the horizontal canopy of the tin-hazel grove, beyond the hedge of closely arranged beach-glass roses.

They continue along the stone path and enter the gallery through a different door, proceeding on to a larger space. It is a sitting room in which all of the furniture is constructed of slightly damp sea-sponges. A placard reads:

Clothing optional. Tea is served to visitors in shell cups.

They peer in to see a woman in a large hat, a slip and heels, elegantly drawing a clam shell to her lips. "She looks practiced" Clara remarks.

Across from the woman in the slip, is the man who emerged from the felt tunnel in shorts.

They disrobe, and enter barefoot in steps which sink slightly.

They sit upon a divan. The sea sponges are relatively warm. "Tell me more about your projects."

"My projects?" Clara asks.

Their tea arrives in opal-hued snail shells carried on an enamel tray.

She begins, "I have been somewhat occupied though not entirely pleased with a series of portraits."

"Portraits of—?" But she pauses realizing that she can ask nothing which she considers to be meaningful, no question, and that what she most hopes is that Clara will speak about her aspirations without reference to any question she might pose. She wishes Clara to begin speaking, and then to continue. But Clara has answered her unfinished question, and briefly.

"Of objects, persons." She raises her shell again.

"I'd like to see them," she answers, somewhat shyly, gazing at the opal hue at the bottom of her empty shell.

"I'm hoping you might do more than to see them." She places her shell down again.

She answers nothing wondering what her friend has meant.

Clara reads her uncertainty and offers, "I hope that you might be persuaded to be a subject."

Amelia falters at this. It was unexpected. But she is not unwilling. "I will, if you'd like." She sets the snail shell aside, pleased despite her tentative attitude. She opens quietness. She waits. She wants to ask something more.

"What occurs despite transparency," she pauses, "I'd like to locate that" she hesitates, "but not to make it still."

Amelia recalls, I am a polite archer with my camera but this says nothing about my "aim" which is often prior to the vision being stabbed.

Clara is speaking through the object surrounding her. The question is open. "I want to learn one aspect of light. Its interior"

An entrance, Amelia wonders. But she says "and aiming at is the emphasis which insists on itself more fluently than any marker."

Again she places her shell down. And then makes a motion as if to stand. Amelia follows. They are given warm towels to dry themselves. They step out across the slightly damp floor, past the pedestal coral tables, the seaweed pressings along the walls. They do not speak now and she is wondering what is entailed in "being a subject." A subject? What is required of a subject of this polite archer? They dress and proceed up a broad staircase.

Amelia runs her hands along the banister covered with feathers. At the landing, they pause in front of a bench constructed of goggles. The lenses are multi-colored.

"This could be very useful," Clara suggests, " an addition to my studio."

"Yes," Amelia agrees, "though will it fit?" They study the sculpture.

"Let us see." She removes her brocade scarf and pulls it across the length of the bench. "Roughly two scarves long," she announces, "half a scarf wide." She stands back.

"And the height?" Amelia asks. Clara approaches the bench again.

"Just shy of one kneecap." They pause, considering.

"It will fit then?"

"Yes. But I don't think I'll take it now." A look is passed between them, as they notice that a few passersby have stopped to watch their experiment, as has a gallery guard.

"No, too much of a bother. It must be very heavy."
She makes a motion as if to lift it.
"Impossible for swimming."
"It would sink."
"Or flying." They look up. "Not streamlined."
"And fragile."
"Difficult to see through besides." They bend their faces down toward the goggles, looking through at various angles. They circle the bench. Then stand from the distance of a few feet taking in the whole of the room.

"Have we then exhausted the afternoon?"
"All of these palaces?"
Another studied step and glance and they are gazing directly at the exit sign. They slowly button their coats.
Amelia returns to the book. "Are you certain she finds her way? I imagined she might linger there end-lessly in the corridor."
"That isn't very kind of you." Clara returns. But now she is gazing at Amelia with a sober air. An imploring gaze she has not before noticed. "It is the only detail I will insist upon."
"To return to the outside?" It seems only fair, Amelia concludes. "So she will," she pauses, and then adds, shifting her tone deliberately, "as we must."
"Beyond the walls of this magnificent enclosure? Shall we?"
"Yes, we must."

They move towards the doors, the bright sunlight and icy cement outside.

The air seemed always in conversation. It had never been mute as far as she could tell but the fall was particularly active. This briskness of walking amidst crinkling leaves and billowing trees, wavy sidewalks, and sidewalk cats. This walking amidst the colors which seemed to recount to her the unreal within the real. This soft red berry, hung glossy between twisted vines. This darkening hip or haw, and definite thorn. The ever present strawberry tree, prolific in it's fruit. The sticky maple treachery all over the cement steps leading home, in a wind which might have been raining yellow, in an air which might have been silver or gruel. The faint presence of rain.

All of this came back to Clara as she opened her door, the city night carried in by her guests, whose flushed expressions partially obscured by masks and wigs were nonetheless present as indicators of a greater gathering. That of the whispering of twigs, and the careful erosion of names. All of this recognition she swept away as carelessly as she closed the door on temporality, knowing that to do so was futile. She greeted her guests gradually, as she was able to recognize them behind their assemblages of papiermache and grease paint. What amused her even more than the night sky with the observatory on her toe, the anatomically correct arachnid and the robed and chained hippogriff, were the titles they had arranged for themselves.

"I am the death of the seasons combined."

"I am Percy Shelley, in the process of being drowned."

"I am the basic principles of epic composition."

"I am the tragic side of tragedy."

She marveled at the display. Swathed in a diaphanous pale cloud of scarves and fabrics, her figure, in itself unpronounced now seemed to vanish amidst her veils. Her cheeks powdered pale, face unmistakably drawn. She said,' "I am that which is most difficult to pronounce."

Amelia perched in a corner, the bill of a swan adorning her features, a glass of emerald held carefully between her webbed gloves. She was caught within corner after corner of mutual apprehension. Gazes driven beyond perception. Numerous persons touched her shoulders and disappeared into distances of foreclosed intercourse. Conversation which she could not surmount. She considered speech as an interlude between silence and silence again. She considered the distance between the sounds of their voices intermingling, and her apparently divisible corner. She watched amiably from beneath a cloud as coats and candles escorted guests. She would soon lie down upon the day bed, upon the forgotten costumes and mislaid pronunciations, the misplaced forward gestures. She would take off her plumage, her divisible silences, and sleep as simply as the most common of breathing isles. As if not a token could have kept her from her eventual dream.

She watched Clara come and go between minuets, between trays of clouded and colored glasses, between capes and attitudes taken off and laid down. Beside her sat a crowned maiden with silver slippers and puffed sleeves. Once this princess had convinced all of her crinolines to bend so that she might sit with hoop down, she had been reluctant to move. Amelia spoke to her, while Neptune and Zeus passed, and then a group of gangsters, and a serious lobster. She felt a bit dreary, a bit drowsy from her pool of emerald spirits, so laid them aside, and the princess had little to recount beyond a collection of guesses as to the best locations for acquiring paste gems (as her gown had required many) and the precarious mechanics of costume devising. She had done this all herself, and the slippers had required dyeing and beading.

As the puff-sleeved maiden continued on to the fascinating subject of the design of one's tiara, quite proudly displaying her work, Amelia's eye was caught by the tail of a very tall leopard, who then whipped around to reveal a blackened nose, whiskers, and the deft and graceful movements which, had they not been inherent, could not have been part of the general effect of the costume. Beside the fact that the cut of his coat, the only one a leopard should wear, the line of his leg quick, the curve of his mouth a particular curl, there was something in his presence unmistakably familiar. She was transfixed with the odd sensation that she must know this person, but seeing him from a distance for a only brief moment had left her guessing. He was soon swallowed up by the backs of an undertaker and several corpses being carried in mock coffins. She heard the light scuffling of his black shoes as he turned and was gone.

She had become so absorbed in marking his progress across the room, that she had failed to respond to the princess's last explanation, even with a nod. Unluckily, this last detail involving her costume had been a confession with which she had wished to unburden herself. Upon finishing her tirade about her sister's extensive collection of paste jewels, all from the turn of the century, and how she had so cruelly refused to lend even the least lovely, which would have matched her gown perfectly, she had taken it upon herself, to borrow that piece, with the intention, to explain, after the fact, when all was safely returned, what she had done.

Having lost the leopard entirely now, and hearing all of this for the second time, with many apologies for her lack of previous attention, Amelia was questioned, had it been her sister who had refused to loan the necklace, would she in her place, have done the same?

She answered truthfully. "But I have no sister."

The princess appeared disappointed at this response and tried to keep her for a moment. She joked, "You'll go in search of one then?"

Amelia shifted her attention back to the necklace. The princess noticed her gaze.

"Isn't it charming?" she asked begging for one small assurance, gently fingering the jet, ruby and pearls encircling her neck. But as the princess reached for Amelia's hand with her own free fingers, to emphasize her speech, she had in so doing tilted her glass of burgundy, which spilled serenely into Amelia's small purse, which dangled from her wrist and had come undone. The wine also spotted her white plumage. She reached into one not as yet drenched compartment and gathered a handful of matches.

Regrets were sincerely offered. Amelia said nothing, but with fair reason to take her leave she stood. The princess was still seated, though in a posture of apologetic gravity.

As she lifted her brow, her gaze no longer slightly grazing the floor, the concentrated tables dimmed. The masks gathered. Moment clasped. Tentacles around backs around chairs. Faces lifted green and ashen. She had vanished into the clamor, and now could no longer glide, as her wings became entrapped within each small flurry of conversation. Backs covered with scales. Golden and crinoline chatter, perceiving, without half looking up.

The clock had begun to lilt, and she found she made faster progress through the crowds with her bill pulled down over her nose. She found Clara, fallen into a basket of rope at the far end of the studio, surrounded by seastar, gull, and anemone. All of their reflections seemed to move towards her, as she approached the obsidian mirror over Clara's head, which had been moved from the hall, and darkened for the occasion. The evening wore on into the morning, with the mirror slightly lightened, and the characters slowly filing out into the wet streets. Until finally only Clara and Amelia remained, looking out the window at the last few costumed guests disappearing, bright against the gray street and mist covered buildings.

CLARA

She tore out the pages, placing them in front of her notebook. Amelia, as she imagined in costume, for the first time theatrically entering the chorus of dimly concentrated tables.

She glided into the room with her reflection diagonally in front of her, parting the carpet with partridges and orchestra.

Across Clara's page, across leagues of social plumage in order to disappear onwards, amidst the scenery. Across the construct of watery minds.

She had once supposed herself to be eloquent. But the room was merely divided where her pen had stopped. It was half as it was, and half as she imagined it, still strewn with remnants from the party.

She looked about her as if remembering this moment, and then continued, with a more angular script, and sought to displace her earlier version, which wasn't exactly accurate.

All things beyond form. A portrait. Where she exists beyond ether.

The fledgling and it's shadow, both present at once.

A Riddle

When one has wool, one has a cap, when one has a sheep one has wool, when one has a spider, one has an angora spider. When one has a cat, what does one have?

Sebastion's Afternoon

He walked out into the day as if it were not raining sun, and with no particular errand, no particle of light. With the deft and graceful movements which, had they not been inherent, could not have been part of his general stride. One does grow tired of waiting. Waiting and raining. As if to be elsewhere or otherwise. As if to be circumspect the ground will interact with it's spectators. He perhaps tries to be less childish and perhaps does not succeed. As the day pours upon the musical memory of chairs, or the pneumonic memory of the Cyclops. No double vision, but perhaps the serrated afternoon.

Perhaps we will save ourselves from the common interest of snail neighborhoods. The vision supposing the vision worn. Too many underclothes is not the same as too many undertakings, and too many undertakers spoil the outing. No discrimination of the dead is pardoned, and yet the dead persist. Perhaps we will save ourselves from the vision preceding the worm. Too many spectators spoil the childish chair. Too many chairs spoil the floor. No double pardon was otherwise beckoned. He fell to the unspoiled sanctuaries of aromatic memory.

Aromatic stopsigns and aromatic pneumonics. He kept himself warm by counting the number of persistent worms. And so on. The necessity of German chocolate Saturdays persists.

She follows him. Changes time of day. It is twilight. He is just passing the steps of a church, around the shaded corner, wall covered with ivy. She is ten paces behind, taking note. His shoes are very black and make an even clicking as he walks, quite rapidly. The corner turns to night, the crowd appears muddy. And now all of the shoes are black, and clicking. Lost in thought in the unfolding dampness, she looks up, but has lost him in a flutter of dark umbrellas pulled out from satchels and lifted. The street is obliterated into a sea of black.

She steps into a cafe, wondering where the tedious streets have led him. Sitting down in a corner. Folding her black bird beside her, shaking off the rain. A steaming cup is placed in front of her. The night set image of the figure disappearing.

Besides his long silhouette, the fluidity of the curve of his mouth familiar. She sat in the twilight. His night then taking place at any time of day, the darkness within the skull surrounding. She wanted to enter his conception of night, his perception, the eyesight amid smaller senses, less color and depth. The spectacle of what has ended, color erased and muddy. So as not to be alone amidst the blackness, which seemed premeditatedly hers. Her diary of matte tones. Her lost thought. What had not been accomplished, thrown hastily within a darkened drawer. The mailing of such, the inside of an envelope. She wished to take with her some semblance of this darkness. This internal dusk, which he carried, singularly his own, so as to isolate their dialogue to the confines of a tête-à-tête. That unlit room held fluttering between this world and that.

His definition of what happens after sunset. His darkening frame. His lamp lighted. The window pressing back along the ridge of perpetually crossing eyes. A frame which has been mapped and measured, this particle of dark water. She wished to walk into this after-dark as all had been orchestrated. She stood there, half certain and half afraid, that when this notion had closed she would find herself a novel midnight. And who, or what can be counted on alongside this growing dimension of foundlessness, formless potential of nothingness, and all of it's sounds?

THE SOLILOQUY OF THE LEOPARD

I had seen her only once, but she insists it was twice, the second time in question while I was out walking in an afternoon which vividly turned to rain. But as I was returning from no particular errand on another such nondescript day, walking through the park which had become frozen, I noticed someone gathering the ice from the backs of the leaves and holding these impressions to the skies. It was a day within which no one paused because of the cold. Yet she stood, almost still, gathering the frozen light within her palms. Carefully placing the ice skeletons within her pockets.

As I approached she looked at me quite oddly, almost not seeing me at first, and then completing all of her movements, stopping abruptly. The leaves of ice melting in her open palms.

The park was passing. The light lifting across her face. Encased in glass. We walked. The day was so bright in it's dullness. Silver streaked. Portent of snow, or was it rain? Clouds pulled across her features, as she questioned. At a glance this pulled me furthest from the measuring out of footsteps between the cold and my destination. Tasks and clocks. The humming of the sidewalk, a chime.

I was stopping to study the light. Museums of frozen foliage. Before the leaves of ice were melting in her open hand, there had been no leaves of ice.

From the first I had vividly turned to rain, walking through a landscape of ice in the depths of a winter which had seemed to pause because of the cold. I had carefully placed my skeleton within the appropriate casings, completing all of my movements, passing with only a vision of dullness, and apparently forgetting to look up.

The park was lifting. Encased in glass. She carried a museum of clocks, as if her silver glance could melt the clouds.

The theater is barely dim enough and every row is filled. A wash of red color suffuses the screen and remains for approximately three minutes during which time the soundtrack is a sort of banjo which reminds one of a red checkered picnic table, sprinklers, or the fourth of July. Nothing is seen upon the screen. Amelia mildly dozes. She overhears, Serrated-Edged-Jaw,

"but there is nothing upon the screen. "

Scalloped-Neck laughs loudly. "Cannot you imagine what images are there"

"Yes, a four cornered table, summer children are running. Cannot you imagine the theater is barely dim enough, a wash of red sprinklers, a sort of screen which mildly dozes."

"Cannot you imagine a chequered wash of running red. Corn dozing off. A large and dusty dog. A sort of banjo or a dimly red theater, or three minutes of this."

Scalloped-Neck, "that's impossible. Clearly, there is no 'nothing upon the screen to be told. Place that before me and I will truly be impressed. Place in front of me a table, place in front of me neckties, place in front of me a four-cornered map. Place in front of me a dusty dog."

The theater is barely dim enough and every row is filled. A wash of red color suffuses the dusty dog during which time a set of sprinklers are set to spinning. Amelia briefly stands, straightens her edges and walks down the aisle to the front of the theater, disappearing behind the screen. She begins to raise her body above the ground. From her standing position, her feet and legs are slowly lifted until she is hovering several feet above the ground, as if lying on her back. Her shadow spills through the screen.

The theater is barely dim and beginning to notice her shadow cast across the depths of red nostalgic nothingness. Her hair and dress dip almost to the ground. Her arms are folded into her chest. Her eyes are closed. Of course no one can see her expression, covered in a wash of red, her entire chest flushed, as the three minutes have nearly ended and she slowly begins to lower herself to the ground and then standing behind the screen she contemplates for half of one thought only, whether or not to return to her seat in the dimly lit theater. The half thought passes, and she has exited through a door behind the screen, not exactly wishing to discuss what no conscious deliberation had precipitated. Most likely she did not wish to learn the effects of her unpremeditated exhibition as she was too very tired to be cross-examined, and so continued on her way home to walk, somewhat carelessly away.

The theater is still barely dim and filled with numerous lisping. The audience assumes some type of cunning on the part of the Sundered-Lip, and he somewhat baffled into silence continues to say nothing. Some were speculating as to why he had chosen Amelia to be part of his piece. Others were jealous. No one could divulge from him the secret as to her appearance. But all had seen her walk behind the screen and rise up. Several studied the space behind the projection room, the stage and the screen, searching for evidence. No ladders or strings were found. No mere hidden curtains or risers. No extra projection. No reflection or optical illusion. This was unusually good, was the overall consensus. And so Sundered-Lip said nothing, and so nothing was said. But "the girl" now referred to by her name more often was suddenly launched into the center of conversation once more, as if she had arrived once again, this time as if her introductions had proceeded her.

———————

Amelia's room was mildly bent. It began to snow. She took to her bed. Sebastion quietly entered the room. He took off his shoes. She was stretched out on the daybed, considering snow upon the wrought iron window bars. He placed before her a bag of steaming soup. A box of tissues. She sat up slowly and examined his face. It seemed to have grown deeper. His eyes set firmly back a hollow darkness which plummeted. He hadn't been there, in the theater, and now he wanted to hear. But another step upon the stair intruded. Another key in her lock. Clara. Lips darting about the room. Nothing serene in her eye. She tripped across the floor in square and heavy toes. And now upon her were four inquiring eyes.

She offered, "I'll tell you the trick."

"But we already know, there was no trick at all."

"Then what is it you'd like to know?"

"Just why you are here in this bed."

"Because I'm ill."

"We can see that."

"Well then, what is it you'd like to know?"

"Just what was it that possessed you?"

"All right, I'll tell you."

"But we already know."

"Then what is it you've come to ask?"

"Why didn't you tell us?"

She clasped and unclasped her hands. Laid her head upon the pillow beside the soup and raised it again. She was in no mood for these visitors, who furthermore had not been invited. She clapped her hands together three times, turned out the lamp, and imagined that they had vanished.

And only then did she venture to answer.

"Why didn't you tell us?" they repeated.

"I did not know myself."

THE DIMLY CONCENTRATED TABLES, AGAIN

They sat at one of the dimmest edges of perception, faces obscured further by the smoke which rose between them. Scalloped-Neck buttoned and somber. Dark-Lash collapsed within a chair. They were tossing back and forth the previous night. "The girl", rising from her seat in the theater. Walking down the aisle, rustling. Rising upon the red screen. Amelia, though they never once mentioned her name.

"There was nothing upon the screen," Dark-Lash began.

"Yes, and then there was." Scalloped-Neck had tired of the preliminaries, but Dark-Lash did not seem to notice.

"There was the shadow of the girl," he continued.

"How did she create this impression?" Scalloped-Neck asked the question, as if assuming Dark-Lash contained the answer.

"A hidden projection, a set of collapsible risers?" He offered uncertainly.

"Place in front of me the projection, place in front of me the risers. Place in front of me the girl herself, answering this, and then I will tell you. I don't wish to know how it was done." Dark-Lash now received the full weight of his intention, but was unable to assist.

"She will not talk if Sundered-Lip would not."

"I had no idea they were conspirators." Scalloped-Neck would now be reading his response to see if it were truthful. Dark-Lash complied.

"Nor had I. He's apparently very secretive at present. He has not returned any messages." He said this and then he set his glass down.

"But coming round again to the question."

"The question?"

"Yes, how they pulled this off without speaking of it? Involving a newcomer without even considering—what was intended? Have you any ideas?" The smoke curled up, obscuring the intensity of his gaze. Dark-Lash studied his possible responses. He could come up with none which satisfied him, and so stabbed at the asking itself. He said nothing.

Scalloped-Neck continued, "The question is immaterial."

"Why is that?"

"Because the matter is finished. If I'd had any ideas, I certainly would not continue to ask." He raised his glass once more.

"Perhaps you have finished it. Perhaps it has not yet begun." Scalloped-Neck studied this last response, wishing to match it in his vagueness. He turned the phrases over again. What was to begin, he wondered. And he concluded there was nothing he had not already seen, only Dark-Lash wandering amid semantics.

"Nothing has begun, except perhaps an interruption. And that will end easily enough. If Sundered-Lip does not see fit to at least inform us, he certainly cannot expect us to uphold his position He must know that. What else are we to think? He has made his choice."

The statement was clear to Dark-Lash, that Sundered-Lip had been determined to now exist beyond the dimly delineated string of tables surrounding them. And largely because he had brought Amelia into it's range, without the knowledge or consent of others. But why did the decision always come down to Scalloped-Neck? To Dark-Lash, it was merely a matter of opinion, not a clear breech. Even though Sundered-Lip had not followed the usual measures before presenting his piece, this sudden unexpected event had the air of enlivenment, perhaps partially since it had enraged their centerpiece. He would not leave the remark unchallenged.

"Wouldn't you call her appearance a deliberate part of the piece? How does that qualify as an interruption?

Scalloped-Neck seemed even more exasperated at this. "He chose to interrupt his work with a distraction. He wasn't bold enough to allow his film to be studied."

Dark-Lash considered. Was it a question of what was beneath the setting, that had not been given room to emerge? He concluded it was not.

Scalloped-Neck continued, "Of course, though the girl is obviously not what she appears. This wasn't her orchestration. She was merely following his carefully plotted course. "

The weight of his words annoyed Dark-Lash, who despised his narrowness. He was obviously trying to trivialize her part. Out of habit he countered.

"She is quite clever," he paused, "from the little I've seen of her."

He watched his companion's expression, "Just how little have you seen?"

Dark-Lash here had to admit, "very little, almost nothing, but she promises—."

"Promises what?" He demanded, positively glaring.

Cut entirely from his purpose in speaking, he had dropped his convictions. As if Scalloped-Neck had torn them from him. He knew the tone only too well. Dryly he replied, "The question is immaterial."

Scalloped-Neck had another pause. "Dare I ask why you choose to use my own words?"

Dark-Lash pondered. "No you mustn't," he replied, knowing he hadn't won.

"All right then." Scalloped-Neck was aware he had been somewhat kind. He was not prepared to brush off yet another member, perturbed at having just lost one. Though unswerving in his manner, he was still willing to test his constancy.

Dark-Lash was relieved, and determined to discover his companion's motives. But once again he was caught off guard.

Scalloped-Neck plunged ahead, giving him little time to consider, "You are interested?" The silence fell between them.

There was no purpose in forestalling. He could not do so successfully. "I did not say I was not. I confess, she does interest me. But it is not so much what she has done."

"What then?" He asked, studying the ash which had fallen from his fingers.

"More what she has not. She hasn't spoken of it since. Hasn't appeared upon the scene."

"Yes, it is odd, isn't it." He was letting himself be led, allowing Dark-Lash to reveal himself.

"And the question that she points to—."

"Does she point to anything at all?"

"Yes, she very clearly questions, as if she herself were a question mark." Dark-Lash was so assuredly certain of this remark, it's obfuscation of his true intent, the way the shape seemed to hang in the air above them, terribly abstract.

"She looks nothing of the sort." Scalloped-Neck hadn't wavered. "You're being absurd," he asserted, his fingers firmly wrapped around his glass. His eyes fixed as if through Dark-Lash directly to the wall behind him.

Dark-Lash held his place simply. "And?" This count of absurdity held no weight with him, still it did pierce a bit, despite his quick return. There had been no venom in Scalloped-Neck's reproach, but it had distracted him enough to leave him with no idea where he himself had been leading the discussion. Scalloped-Neck was still one league ahead.

He placed the question firmly. "I'm wondering if she will make such a display again."

He leapt to reply. "If she is capable of defying gravity once, she is most likely capable of doing so again."

"Are you suggesting that you believe this girl is able to—" They both paused and momentarily laughed.

Dark-Lash had been circling the question, so he thought, silently. But he had been heard. He had allowed himself to luxurize in the faint possibility. He didn't believe it of course. Wouldn't harbor any mystery of the sort. Wouldn't be seen in public with such a look upon his face. He felt as if he'd been found wearing a distinctly ugly coat at the most notable event of the year.

Scalloped-Neck knew this, but he could see Dark-Lash had succumbed to the possibility of the unreal; the realm in which she appeared to dwell, but could not possibly have existed. And to consider this realm was decidedly out of the question.

His only escape was to turn it around once more. To deflect the subject from his private musings, and to point it more towards the philosophical. He brushed away the unpleasant mirage and proceeded, as if unlooping his foot from a snare.

"And if she did have the ability would you consider that an art?" He said this with a comic emphasis, weighing his doubt against his smugness.

"That is the question she makes of herself? I doubt this very much. It is no question at all. How to consider something so unlikely?" Dark-Lash by now, had recovered his footing. He had returned to that unwritten code of considerations based upon which his place at this table existed.

"Precisely, " he replied, "it isn't worth considering."

As we walk now through the passing park she speaks nothing of it.

"What shall I say about it?" she might answer.

When I ask her to explain how she has done this she wonders to what it is I refer.

It is from her account of all things as if her body had been lifted. Her own legs carried her to the surface. It may have been her motion alone, but from where it has sprung she seems unable, or unwilling to reply.

Something has been stolen from her account. Not as if she were withholding, but as if someone were withholding from her. As if a secret key could be placed before her and then she would be able to explain how she has arrived at this time and place, and why she has been given the ability to rise.

She seems intent on shrouding the event with lattices, with puddles and quiet gaze. As if it were only a story she were telling, which involved another.

"But it is another" she might say. "Another aspect of the story anyone tells, which is illusory."

I consider all acts of flight. I consider fancy. I consider the unknown. Her airblown fingers. Her ethereal smile. Could it be the secrecy of the delineated string of tables, which I supposed she had merely brushed by with the faintest acquaintance? Could it be her allegiance to another? A game of chance? Could it be something within the correlation of several weather systems?

There is nothing to be said to myself, as she would say, except what is told. So action excludes speech. Speech is also action and precludes itself beyond the tense in which it has arrived.

Her softest glance falls upon me. It is not her movement which perplexes but the tumult of all those around her. She walks transfixed among her onlookers, steadily, as if suspended from generous billows of fabric wafted quickly into the air. And all around her lose their footing.

SUNDERED-LIP

If he were to speak, he would have spoken here, but he did not. He did not stop to ask how she had accomplished her display. He did not wonder why she had chosen his work, or the particular hour. He did not speak to anyone including Amelia, who nonetheless, he considered to have ruined his piece. He averted his eyes when she approached, considered her existence solely as an intrusion, and begrudged her further still, her sudden and constant appearances within quarters he had formerly assumed to be his own. He did not stop to consider that the majority present at the performance, excluding of course a good part of the chorus, thought this to be his most impressive accomplishment to date. He also did not comprehend, that perhaps she had done him a very large favor. He stood in silence, until the time within which he might have spoken had passed. Then, from what he considered a safe distance, he resumed his usual speaking as if nothing at all had occurred. He was aware that for some his silence had surpassed boundaries, over which he would not be permitted to recross, so he quietly stalked these perimeters in his comings and goings, unaware that his legs had publicly betrayed him, when his motives in walking had only been to carry himself away.

Clara

Amelia discussed the incident to no ends with Clara, by the light of her pink lamp, while the street below the studio rushed into evening, and the kettle was lit numerous times. Clara replied that if one were not to act imprudent in one's youth, when else could one dare? One had to set a precedent at some point to toss conventions aside. She encouraged her to stage perhaps a still more audacious plot.

Clara also had the advantage of distance. She had not been present in the theater, she had not followed Amelia about in the flurry of commotion which followed, she had not heard any of the gossip and was barely aware of the others involved. She knew at a glance exactly what Amelia had been dealt, a blow from a dim chorus who wished to explain the inexplicable.

It was understood between them that Amelia possessed a manner of persuasive gravity. Clara was never astonished, not being one to doubt that the inexplicable was marvelous as it was, and even more marvelous untouched.

AMELIA

The thought had traveled widely from the tips of her fingers up to her shoulders, but originated most likely within the eyes, which first fell upon the vision as if it were some brilliant gift, the presence of one or more other bodies of intelligence. They surrounded her, rapt with her performance. They radiated, and she was suddenly swept. The next she knew, thought had become inflamed, and moved slowly, continuously, leaving a hideous trail across her once perfectly clear reflection. Her once countenance. And her once complexion. This was unfair, but the dream continued on until she might lean too far across a table, open her eyes too widely, or fall upon the arm of another. Suddenly fondness became nearness, and the nearness of one, when another was not, became the desire to lay her head easily onto anyone's shoulder, as if her desires were as transferable as anyone's wish. She knew that none of this was true, as a phantom tooth is not true, and yet that illusory nature contained and compelled her. Conversation became a stunning lure, and the night a terrible pendant, which swung before her, somewhat dazzling, and quite whole. Quite intact. Quite complete, unlike herself she supposed. These first wrecking stages of rumination were played continuously, until she might fall exhausted upon a chair or a couch, or even better a bed, to begin all again the culmination of sleep to which she was ultimately driven. She was ultimately persuaded to lie down with any idea amid her bedding. Any little thought would do. And thought contains thought, continues to desire nothing. It was this nothingness which was transferable as anyone's wish, not the shoulder, or her eyes which opened again as charms, and reminded her of all that she saw. The world came into existence once again as it had one reddish night, when her entire existence had been suspended, and no other thought had been permitted near her. This was nothing like that. This was a small guarded island of thought which she kept separate from the rest.

She was unmistakably drawn to that one who all considered her conspirator, that one who routinely avoided her eye. But to speak of it, to record it seemed almost as unpardonable as to think, since to record was to recognize.

It is my faulty perception again, she thought. Newness of new exchange humming. It isn't really anything like being unveiled. Nothing like the desire to couple. All of this and much less. Nothing like the notion to fawn, to fall upon one's senses, to seek pleasure for pleasure's sake.

She sought a subtle kind of intimacy which is often lost as certain mechanisms in the most intricate clock. All parts continue to move. We have soiled nothing if we ourselves are not sullen. We lose something like the unmistakable dawn. It has little to do with skin, but all to do with complexion.

She sought the cultivation of thought as a real substance, which could carry her through the long stretches of uncultivated soil upon which she lavished her attention. All of the untrained meaning which was the very pleasure of the language itself. It was this exchange of dimness like the exchange of letters, or assurances which had come to confuse her mechanisms of thought. So that she stood wondering who could ever be trusted with such a secret. The sensuality of thought when given over to one who was wanted as an accomplice. An accomplice, not to possess, but to postulate, and pass the many hours tossing over their aspects.

And as the law in these parts of subliminal speech, certain segments remain locked, and others unhinged. She had checked her mechanisms nightly to find a disturbed sequence of doors and windows, complicated shutters and blinds, and borrowed books of incantations which might control everything, if one had the purpose and the notion to concentrate upon their fittings. If one could simply bear down upon a postulate something would give. The soil of her thought would turn. In a hospitable environment, even the irreparable may recover with little wound.

Even so, it seemed not quite right to invite such distances into one's heart, such miscalculations into her personal mythology, which somehow had not allowed for the need of such costly bearings. She thought then that possession of self-knowledge would solve the lost shore. But she was late in asking. In all of her grazing upon the scenery, she had dropped the thread, barely could claim a memory of her movements. She contained no privileged insight, almost as if someone else had completed her actions. This was the unenviable distance. She burrowed further into forgetfulness, noting the disturbed sequence of mechanisms, resolving to return at a later time and find them unlatched.

The later time did not arrive as she had expected. It did not saunter or dally, gently suggesting her return. Instead she was confronted directly with faltering and insinuating lapses. She stumbled at last upon the final and most elaborately barricaded tower, and to her surprise found it unguarded. With a few simple orchestrated steps she had stepped across a threshold. She now stood within a measure of her own breath. What she learned surprised her greatly—that her unwilling conspirator all along had no intention of speaking. He did worse than not to question her meaningfully as she had hoped. What she had imagined once to be his interested gaze purposefully grazed the floor or the ceiling each time she passed. And beyond this, the atmosphere surrounding his presence seemed to emit hostility, though his lips had not come near enough speech even to shudder. She had perhaps wrongly chosen. She was not sure why she had been so bold. She did not expect gratitude, or even politeness, but what she did hope might ensue from her actions was a meaningful engagement. She knew she had been perhaps rash to intrude in the manner that she had, but she was severely taken aback to realize, once the initial interest in her as a new presence had settled, that for the most part she had not been taken seriously by the one she had most hoped to reach.

This was not all that she saw when the last series of doors unbolted and opened before her. There she found the deft and graceful movements of another more willing companion, whose costume she immediately recognized. She had least expected this. She had not meant to relegate him to these unmanageable turrets. She had not meant to remember him here, so near. It was almost a personal affront. She had no idea by what means he had entered. She vowed to herself that his friendship must not be forsaken again. That anything less than loyalty would result in the loss of a companion who seemed to linger in the very depths of her own reticent oracle.

THE ACCIACCATURA OF AMETROPIAN POGONIPS

As pink skies became smudges and trees silhouettes. There was a light, and a globe and she sat within a composition notebook imagining crickets, a large bouquet of lavender, as if lavender could be anything but diminutive. Such was the night. A voice lilting across water. Or so she thought. There was a knock at the door.

Clara. Clouds in a vase of bergamot. As soon as she opened the door a seaplane happened by. Complexion clear as translucent glass. But then looking below the skin, she saw her premise. They were to go, and before the name of the place had escaped her lips they were in route towards the Academy. She followed alongside her. Simultaneously they walked. Clipped sharp steps upon the cold cement.

Amelia, a short grace note one half step below a principal note, sounded immediately before or at the same time as the principal.

Amelia, sustained dissonance.

Approaching the subway, a dense fog of suspended ice particles, especially obscuring a particular fruit stand.

The walk seemed without measure, a dense fog, a half step behind the sharp clipped premise. Clouds in a vase of something diminutive.

They approached a pale gray building, stepping upon a landing of steps, one on top of the other piled at once precariously, poured perhaps one-hundred years before their arrival. The building lurched out of the fog as if it had not existed before. Amelia had passed it's pale heavy windows, perpetually lit up, upon so many occasions, but had never thought to enter it's premises.

Clara smiled upon a gray door, a dense woman in blue jade and large spectacles behind a blue-gray, dun looking countertop, birds in cages around the edges of the room, but what Amelia saw most poignantly was a large rose painted upon the floor of the small room which she largely desired to place her foot upon. She was about to do so, in fact had made a motion to leap, when the eyes behind the spectacles drowned. The figure behind the counter rose monumentally. Clara placed a cautioning hand upon her shoulder, and steered her clear of the room.

But what is it?

But what?

The rose upon the floor.

Yes, the rose. One mustn't step upon the rose.

A cloud in a vase of vapors, traveled down the gray-dun fluid hallway again in a clipping meter upon the polished floors of ever so many grains painted gray. Again, Amelia, a short grace note behind. Another door, this one though burnished, a type of bronze looking wood. A checkerboard floor, black and white. A small room, crowded. There was an elderly man, at once benevolent, sitting upon a stool. The walls covered with books. Half a dozen persons sat on similar stools, holding books upon their laps. The man approached Amelia, pointed to a volume upon a shelf. She recognized none of the names upon the spines.

You begin here, he said, seeming to fade in and out of focus, as if she had been looking through a moving lens. The hazy figure handed her the book, which she took without question.

She held the volume in her hand, it's weight considerable, perfectly fitting within her palm. All of it's pages were covered in gold. Images fluttered as she turned them. The text was small and dense and seemed to shift as she tried to focus. In one sense the book was flat, but in another, it was bird. She did not recognize the alphabet. Though she somehow had understood: the cartographer is the smuggler. She looked up, frustrated, to see Clara had joined the semi circle of others upon stools and benches, holding books upon their laps. They all held pens, and were commencing to sign their names within the books, alongside other names. Amelia thought that she should sign her book as well.

Oh no, the man intercepted, you must read it first.

Clara later drew her aside. Once you have read and signed all of the books within this room, then you may enter. Amelia blinked, looking around at the thousands of volumes, with golden pages, perched upon the well-kept shelves.

Is it possible to take the books home to read, she asked.

That depends, answered the benevolent man, for some will ask repeatedly and the answer is unmistakably no. And others might only suggest, and the books are carefully wrapped and given over.

Amelia, slightly bemused, and uncertain, tried to smile vaguely. She traversed the length of the room in five steps to look out of a double glass porthole, and saw all around, the ocean crashing majestically. The path which they had taken to reach the building had been washed away almost completely. She glimpsed two dark coats, apparently persons within, attempting to cross, with great difficulty, what had once been the street. She turned to Clara.

How will we return?

Clara regards her, recognizes beneath the pondering. She understands the world as a laboratory. A crusade against silence. She remembers her borders, an understudy, a dark dress, drab posture, trappings, waifishness, a little ship of a thing.

Amelia, meanwhile misses the street across the street. The little cafe. Spearmint and lemon. She imagines this to be a very serious undertaking. The rose, betokened. Out the window, a large net rises from the icy waters, covered with earth.

Again, Amelia questions, how to return home?

But Clara is in conversation saying, when writers "discuss" they tend to "run on."

Was that clouds in a vase? Sky, blankets of sky. Her face is so open. But then Clara turns to, and answers gravely:

The night actually is never a consensus. More like a drawing room, and a shutter, and a sparrow, or a lamp which halfheartedly stutters, and then it will be morning.

She saunters towards the door.

If she were told a story, she might become otherwise, no longer emptied.

Amelia follows, noticing, how this part of town has lapsed from her vocabulary. The cartographer is the smuggler.

She's gained some livelihood, and lost some.

Comfort, what is, remarked the sparrow. Remarked the falling disposition. An arrow marked, a lark's desire. The fragrance upon the skirts of the rose.

THE PORTRAIT: TWO IN REFLECTION

They stand looking into a hallway mirror, together, in Clara's studio.

The image is memorized, exchanged for black and white.

Later, they look at the photographs of themselves together. A similar difference, with the exception of color. They look at each other again, see what was not held in glass or frame. Light and shadow remain firm, say nothing.

They stand looking into a hallway mirror. The corridor leads them backwards, clasps and unclasps time. When they move away the place where their feet once pressed into the floorboards is marked. Holds an indentation.

The image is memorized. The corridor waits. They look at each other again. They sit on a day bed, holding the photographs on their laps. Looking down, looking up.

The corridor moves away. Glossy. The photographs look up. The day bed tilts. A similar difference remains. A hallway is exchanged for light. An image exchanged for time.

Their eyelids flicker. The frame shifts, with the exception of color.

Part Two:
The Corridor

Time itself is querulous
privilege of form
A false or drenched derivation
— Lyn Hejinian

She enters the studio and uncoils. There she sees the tilted silhouette. A kitten banished in a corner. Clara calmly adrift, sitting, holding her knees to her chest upon a tattered ottoman, her face close to an old sea chest piled on top of a crooked cabinet of drawers. Her face holds a shadow Amelia cannot surmise. And as she approaches, the figure in the chair seems to kindle. Turns towards her, face awash, a silver kit of rain. But there is no wishing otherwise, no lost within sways. The face remains open. The tears have taken no compromise, have not shrunken her features, or distorted her color. They simply embody, as the silhouette stands; the room as through thick wavy glass seems to sigh.

Amelia steps towards the figure, but as she approaches near enough to touch, the rain vanishes. There is not a trace of the former rivulets. Not a stain upon her face. Has she seen this or has she not?

They go about tea and conversation. Tea and the speed of the afternoon. All the while though Amelia has not lost the burrowed distress. She merely steps upon the trailing ends of some evaporating sorrow, and continues to conjecture all the afternoon long, what has brought this unveiling, then hidden it as minutely.

She lolls, a tilted lingering. She holds out her hand, and the face which turns towards her is bright. The day is dry. Filtered green light. An optical illusion. The room again a poor prescription. Her eyes struggle to find a point of focus. The image remains clear. Clara, upon a tattered ottoman. The delicate rules forbid Amelia to ask. Was she, or was she not, when she heard the step of her visitor's shoe? The day is bright and the trail ends of a passing storm have already scrolled beyond the depths of the studio windows. They go about their afternoon and tea. Who could ever explain this brightness? The spoiled velvet of the old cushions upon which they sit beside the wood stove. Woolen stockings curve into v's, as knees bend and heads lilt upon pillows.

"What did I see, across your face?" Amelia asks.

Hesitation crosses her lip. "A cloud, a windmill of sorts?"

"Why a cloud?"

Clara answers, "It is not here that I belong." The moment is stretched. Dissolves.

"And where is not here then?"

She reaches for another cup. Unbends her knees. Rises up from the cushion. "Elsewhere" she replies.

She tries a lighter tone. "Where light is equal to sound?"

"I don't know myself." Again the moment crystallizes. Falls. "I'll not be far."

Amelia is considering far as a relative term. "Far from twilight?"

The wood stove puffs. A heavy perfume. Diagonal afternoon. The light moves across drying underclothes strewn over backs of chairs. The tea things at their toes. They bend their heads together.

"If you were to board a train—"

"If I were to board a train?"

"From what would you be disentangling?" There is a tautness in her asking.

"Departure is not that."

"The picture moves away."

She looks out the window now, already transparent. "I am being carried somewhere."

She will not pause at the peculiarity of 'carried.' Carried by whom? But her pause is not long enough. She must continue in their shared language. "With a cape and a dictionary—."

"And a camera."

"Did you notice, the way they intertwine? Clara Amela, and Amelia Clare."

"That isn't my name.

"Yes, but," Clara pauses, "since you won't tell me—." Amelia interrupts, "I have."

"It's too ridiculous. Amelia Clarina Simonetta—"

"A lovely invention. Does it please you?"

"Either a mistruth or a misjudgment. You shall be always Amelia-Clare, Bellisima Amelina."

"You've hidden something."

"Then something is hidden."

"Tell me truthfully, was your father really consumed by a beast?"

She considers from what she would be disentangling. "Tell me truthfully, whose father was not?"

The question hangs in the air. Whose father was not? There are beasts, and then there are beasts. She must agree.

Amelia walking home. A breech. A certain seal has been broken, and now unhinged she walks, as if a dull attempt to row against the pavement, she finds herself suddenly bothered by a bird, or a spider or a tendril about her neck. She finds herself somewhat betrayed by her own motion. The street veers away from her very step. Clara has been secretive. There are beasts and then there are beasts. Yes, but since you won't tell me—. The past is mandatory, and she sees herself as a two dimensional figure, flitted around by this or by that. Only a mother of rubble and a father consumed by a beast cannot be believed, precisely. Which is less true or more true? Has she lived on an island with sandalwood horses? Has she grown up holding the hand of a scarecrow?

She reaches home and looks out the window. She changes the season that easily. And that easily she has invented herself. She has invented her present and past no differently from any other. But she has undone the precious passage which leads between herself and her composition. She walks between the orderly lined rows, spilling ink as she proceeds. She does not explain.

She has dispelled the myth which is her name, which is no myth at all, except that she believes none of it. Though she has been led to the evidence, though she has seen with her very clear eyes, with no lack of certainty, her own beginnings.

AMELIA

If we were to walk upon the rose, the stalk, the undernetting, pinnings, crinoline, amidst sunlight. There is too much light in this day. And so I become appalled, or dizzy. The dizzy nest. Between story and character whose black shoes interpose. Alphabet sunrise, a soup gathered towards the sheets. I wanted to draw the curtains around myself, and to drawl. Rehearse hungers and stars. Rehearse the hanging of a vessel to a sun. Mixed understudy sky.

Cardamom rose water morning. Visible rain. Moving forward, we, the obvious backwards, we the mailman reversed. Mail supposes treasure. To motion nowhere. Whose phrases blink. If a moment had waited, had hesitated. What will follow the rain? There is no rain. Where labor is a star as fitting. I will gather my self in two's and three's. They come upon tridents. From a wandering menagerie. They come selling the trinkets beknown to men as mice. They come willingly and often. Until four o'clock. Distraction.

I try to sense the largeness of the day, it's catch and many emblems. I reside within the long breadth of it, not the frayed edges, it's shadow. To avoid the gape. How to think only with the window being dragged down the hill? To stand outside from the span of complete lightness, to complete dark. Seams of darkness drop a richer dye, washed in a sink of yielding color.

It is so tempting to awaken within a new evening, so tenderly unveiled, drawn down and over the senses. All is violet, an orchestration of clouds. The darkness drops. We wandered and watched the fountain change colors five more times. Recall being seated within a vase of color, which dripped absentmindedly. I might glance out and see red, and seeing red realize it is time. Or seeing red, see the end of effort. The moment changes colors. The darkness drops. Consciousness relinquishes hold.

There is a bottle of red, or a claret of a voice, or a pillow of an afternoon.

A glance upon wandering color, a dance upon an absent map. A book has been closed. An insurmountable hour has been summoned. I have motioned to the wind many times, a transition of mind, often referred to as the rotation of a planet upon which we find it convenient to reside.

CLARA'S PORTRAIT

Her breath under glass, as supposition, inhalation cold, exhalation flat, stillness. Water caught in reflection.

Clara, the vanishing, where she remains as vapor. The other half of Amelia's labyrinth missing. She drifts to sleep eventually, her night, full, intact, pressed against her skin as cold cabbage. When a person is heard and not seen. Day smears into night, or a window darkens. Footsteps overhead.

Dusk. The light changes as she shifts rooms. From unlaced persimmon to mild pear.

Dusk + lip = carriage.

The gold arriving between trees as a premonition. The globe of a yolk. Hidden inside a crest. The air was never metered before this turning. The hemispheres of a house are painted upon her robes.

A room can never be insolent. Rows of sleeping books. Behind the privacy of curtains, he unveils to her his proof of the season, a gift of two leaves. One bronze, the other canary. Delicately frilled edges. She turns them over in her palm. The color limpid. Opaque.

Perhaps they are none other than dross. All other leaves have long ago left home. The ground is frozen. There is no one else in the room. The room was never, before this turning, empty. The hours of waiting for night have ended. She does not grace the ceiling. Rows of sleeping leaves. Promises are painted upon her upturned palms. One dust, the other ash. They drift. She rises and sets out. As if she had been encased within glass. A song flung towards a mirror may easily sing back.

THE PHOTOGRAPHS

Where is Clara of the labyrinth? Clara of shadow. Her studio vacant. It has been weeks perhaps. One half of her heart is dull. Disappears. She has received no letter, no forwarding address. She must ask. How much time has passed? She looks into the glass one more time, sees nothing, wonders aloud. She studies the photographs to see if any expression has changed. They remain still in their places.

She approaches the dimly concentrated tables. Clasping as she does the small black portfolio. The only trace of her she clasps. She walks and the street participates. The dimly concentrated tables surmise. Her secret is not found out. She is an oddity. She begins to ask.

"Clara-who? "

Scalloped-Neck tilts askew. Sundered-Lip and Dark-Lash smile as if to remove her.

"Clara-who?" Repeated like a dance or an elk. Amelia nods and sits. Oddly clasps the portfolio. She must ask. The only trace of her clasping as she does. The only trace of her an oddity. One half of her blotted labyrinth. Heavy participles engage her throat.

Dark-Lash submits to ask, "what is that you are carrying?" High-Forehead echoes the request. The request has been taken from her hands, the black book. It is spilled open upon a table. The images persist.

"This one, this one" prods Scalloped-Neck, "In this one there is a strong resemblance."

"Where did you find these?" demands High-Dark-Eye?

"To whom do they belong?" asks Sundered-Neck.

Amelia looks up, all wrong, away from the images to see Scalloped-Eye, High-Lashes, Sundered-Neck. They have all been transposed. She tries to retrieve the pictures.

They toss their questions in multiples, which become hardly discernible.

"How did you come across these?" three falter at once, crowding.

"The-e-s-e" asks another, pointing down.

"Where did you find—wheredidyoufind? The portfolio. Port Olio.

'Port Olio?' she wonders.

"Folio!" demands one, and then a second.

"Polio! Polio!" she hears.

"Are they originals?" another echoes.

"Of course. Of course they are," she hears herself say, "they are—" she answers. She has been saying this to herself. And now she begins aloud. "She gave them to me herself."

The voices suddenly stop.

Amelia sees double. All of them awash. Sundered-Lash comes into focus, pulls her aside. Her certainty mildly collapses.

He begins cautiously, "where did you find these?"
"These are portraits which have been given to me."
"Who gave them to you?"
"The artist. I've already said." She studies his gaze, more and more certain she should not have asked here. Port Olio.
"Who is the artist" he asks slowly, so there might be no mistaking.
"Clara—"
"Clara-who?"
His expression is waiting. "Amela—. Clara Amela."
His expression falls somewhat. His brow troubles her suddenly. His eye, looking for something.
"You knew her—then?" he continues, with a suspicious neutrality in his tone.
"Knew her? Of course" she replies, "of course I know her.
"Know her, still?" he asks. Something is wrong about his shoulders. His fingers clasping the edge of the table. "You must have been very young when she gave these to you."
She looks at him without understanding at all. Very young? She wonders. Am I not very young?

The room begins to tilt. Clara Amela. The photographs spill out onto the floor.

"When did she give you the photographs?"

"Just last week."

He pauses abruptly. Then he laughs. She can make no sense of it. He looks away towards the others. Their backs are turned towards them politely, but he knows they must be listening. Must have heard.

She looks up at him. He has disbelieved her. She is about to stand.

He stops her. "Wait," he insists, placing a hand on her shoulder. She looks at the unwelcome hand. He pulls it back. He has managed to calm his features. But it is a forced display, she is aware.

She looks up into his face again, but this time it is as if her face has revolved through another world. It isn't bright exactly, but somewhat hopeful. He knows something, she thinks. He must. "You know her?" she asks. "Have you heard any news of her?"

He draws back in his seat. His voice is barely audible now. "I knew her very little, years ago."

Years ago, the phrase echoes through her features, leaves an impression. "Have you not seen her since?"

Her question, so innocent. Her question circles about his neck, strains his features terribly. Finally he manages to speak. It is not without some sorrow, not without a slight trembling of his expression which she wonders at. It is not without considering her response. "There must be some mistake. Are you certain?" he asks reaching out towards the portfolio.

Amelia recoils slightly. She is aware that he has asked this question as if he were expecting a confession. "Yes, I'm certain." She responds, firmly clasping the object in question.

"I'm sorry," he says, seeing her agitation, "it's just—. I don't know how to tell you. There must be some mistake." He stops abruptly.

Abruptly some mistake in Port Olio, she thinks. "What is it?" she asks. Still uncertain.

"It's no use if someone has put you up to this—" he finally says. "I recognize them—the photographs. We all do, don't you see?"

She pivots downwards. Folds into her chair. "See what? What is it?" She can barely remain in her seat. The entire room appears flushed.

But he is going on now, tentatively, "Clara Amela, the photographer, whose photographs you have—" he pauses, shifts his gaze again. She thinks the room shivers. "Clara Amela" he continues, "has been dead for ten years."

She says nothing. It isn't possible to speak since the room begins to spill. It begins with the corners moving closer. The angles shifting. Her eyes have difficulty focusing. The room is so warm. She understands none of this. "What do you mean?" she asks. He has not heard her. She supposes that she has not spoken loudly enough. She forms the words. They seem to hang in the air. The corners now collapse entirely.

The floor begins to lurch. She hears dimly in the background, beginning to recede, "yes, that one, it does look much like her, that one 'two in reflection.' " She dimly hears.

Tables and chairs slide across the room. Glasses tilt. Nobody else sees this. They see nothing. Understand nothing.

Clara Amela has been dead for ten years.

She understands, this isn't seeing herself either. The resemblances, in the photographs. They do not breathe, but neither can they be drowned. They possibly do not move, but they have spoken, and all have listened.

They try to gather her up. She must have fallen. She tries to gather her skirts. They are all reversed again, Sundered-Neck, and Scalloped-Eye. They walk her towards the door. Clasping. The photographs have been gathered, from the tilting floor.

She is suddenly encased within glass. Those hands supporting her shoulders do not touch her. As she walks away the conversation dimly recedes.

They have all become impossible. She has seen nothing at all. They do not exist.

The street switches back and forth like railroad tracks, stitches in black. This goes on for days she supposes, though she fails to count. Proof of the season. Ice clings to her heels.

She will travel if she must. The street fixed with the litter of falling minds. Bodies sleeping upon pavement. Ice against her shoe. The season will not relent.

She promises: I will disbelieve history if I must. It will be possible to find you.

The street switches back and forth, frames in black. Time clings to her heels.

She renounces the road. She falls over the wing-tips of her vision which see in all dimensions at once. Her feet pressing down upon the air beneath them, which carry her home. The street spins away, and her handkerchief, (if she possesses one) divides into tears. There is no rain, but she hears the rain falling. Sees a map of rain fallen upon the line which falls behind her.

Home is a vacant construct. Home once meaning the back of her hand. The phrase which keeps repeating inside her plummeting thought has no weight in itself. A scaffolding where the present drops away.

Clara Amela has been dead for ten years.

She dons a train, and travels towards the middle of the city, across a flight of white cement stairs, back. Again, the building seems to jut out of the fog just as in her dream, as if it had not existed before. There is no fog this time, but the building again lurches out from it's peripheries as if not to be missed. Clouds in a vase of mistakes. The glass windows are not translucent. Clipped sharp steps upon cement. She walks a short pitch ahead of herself.

The diminutive woman in blue jade and large spectacles behind the dun countertop smiles mildly. The birds have not yet been awakened. Heavy cloth covers their cages. There is no rose upon the floor.

She travels down the gray-dun fluid hallway again, upon the polished floors, looking for the burnished door, the checkerboard floor, the benevolent man. She finds no porthole, no sea storm, no small white room. No entrance to the rose.

The walls shift pale yellow. She sits at an empty table in front of a flickering screen, typing very hesitantly. The screen appears to cough, and then replies three times to her inquiries. She follows the coded message through a labyrinth of halls and rooms where she observes stools and benches, persons holding pens, and books upon their laps. Finally a brown door, a small room with barred windows. Looking out she sees two persons in very large coats, attempting to cross the street, which is covered with ice. A man is shelving volumes. He does not look up. Amelia runs her hand along a row of books at eye level, searching for the title until its spine reaches her fingertips.

She holds the volume in her hands, it's weight considerable. She sits, remembering her borders. The physicality of the room. The pages come into focus. Fingers search until they arrive. She reads:

—

Clara Amela, born 1966 in Oddly, Connecticut. 1971-84 Attends public schools in Oddly. 1984-1988 attends The Interiors School of Photography, graduates with honors. 1988 moves to 9th Street Studio. Disappearance, 1990.

Exhibitions

1988 April. "One Polite Archer" Capital Letters Center for Photographic Arts

1989 March. "The Emerald Bottle" Constructions Gallery

1991 January. "two in reflection" Museum of Fine Arts

—

She looks at the photograph. Sees herself. She stops reading, drops the volume. Again the walls change tone. The day pivots. The floor spins away. She is walking. It is the year 2001. Something odd about the millennium.

The street appears in waves. She is sitting upon a bench, surrounded by pigeons. She repeats the phrases:

To disbelieve history if I must.

The premise. The rose, one mustn't step upon the rose. But the skirts of the rose?

Night is not usually a consensus.

The rose disappears. The hallway disappears. The bench disappears.

The days appear in waves. At a glance they are flutterings. She does not recognize their alphabets. She dimly hears the background beginning to recede.

This isn't seeing herself either. Encased within glass. The present becomes a theorem. She avoids the dimly concentrated tables. She avoids all glances.

That leaves her only the birds, and the maze. The days and the light.

She remains following the smallest slips of possible traces. The breath of the photographs under a lamp. The small trails of fragrance pressed into her rooms. Her expressions etched there, marveling in a doorway.

AMELIA'S DREAM OF THE CORRIDOR

Sometimes it's the music ending abruptly which convinces me, other times the thermostat which is stuck. And still at other times the portraits on the walls seem to lengthen, but only when I walk through the corridor. Sometimes it is the letters which she writes but does not send, and how they accumulate in precarious piles. The candles burn unevenly and I'm not sure to whom the house belongs or why I am here at all. I go through the closets and try on various attire. I was glad to find both galoshes and sunhat because the weather is so variable.

At one end I might look out and see a blizzard in progress. The snow coming down with such fierceness and speed it seems the house will soon be smothered. Then I might traipse to the other end of the house, drawn by a sound of crashing where I see the surf of the ocean pounding on the glass. The air warm through the glass, as if I could touch it. Then I might wonder about the dimensions of the house, it's length in particular. Since it seems to encompass several weather systems at once. Either way, the house is surrounded by storms. This is a region of dense precipitation. And I dare not step outside most of the time, but am comforted by the provisions I've found.

I've searched for a structure to this disarray. There, upon a stair. I might proceed up, running my hand along the smooth dark banister which seems to hum. At the landing I turn and enter a room on the right. There I see myself enfolded in a bed. My breath seamlessly wandering amid perfumes wafting in the chamber. I measure myself in the pool of sleep. I am convinced it is I. Long velvet curtains have been drawn back. The room is filled with light. Even so it is cold.

I turn away from the figure and step towards the window. But where am I absolutely? The day's brightness? The shadow of snow? I am oddly displaced seeing myself there, as if I might be disturbing the figure. From the distance appearing between us, I might have stepped out onto the vast plains of the tundra. My sense of the house, what little I have gathered, collapses. The compass appears uncrossable.

But then I stand away from the window and look back at the bed. The sleeping figure has vanished.

I turn again and notice an envelope with it's seal broken lying upon the dresser. I lift it and pull out a heavy creme colored card, engraved with the following invitation.

The various "shes"
come together
at noon
for tea
the sitting room.

I wonder what time it is and find a clock by the bedside. It's face red with faint bronze numbers. Eight o'clock. I stretch out on the bed and study it more closely. To my surprise, what I thought to be the second hand, judging not by it's size, but by it's rapid movement, is indeed the hour hand. In what has seemed to me not more than a moment it has made one complete revolution. Nine o'clock. Disbelieving I continue to gaze. Ten o'clock. I leap up, realizing, at this rate, I'll be late for tea.

Where is the sitting room? I run down the stairs and into what seems to be a parlor. Everything is green. Out the windows I glimpse a frozen sedge along brackish waters covered with small lanterns. I pass through into a long hallway where portraits on the walls appear to lengthen as I near them. It might be their eyes follow my gaze. I look away and hurry through to the other end and find myself in the kitchen. Possibly, more than one kettle is whistling. A woman with an apron over a russet gown clicks into the room in pointed shoes and begins arranging the tea service. She turns to me and asks if I will carry a tray. I follow her back down the hallway with the portraits, which do not misbehave in her presence. We come out into a large dining room which I had not noticed before. She places the tray at the end of the table, and then asks if I'll be needing anything more. It might be the way that she asks the question each time which draws a boundary between us. This surprises me since the tea service is for several, and I assume that she will be joining me. There is no one else in the room. She laughs.

"Oh", she answers, "I must be getting along. Another storm is expected." I look towards the bright windows and see a serenely blue sky.

"The other guests—" I broach, as she turns to exit the room.

"I expect they are all sleeping" she answers. Then she turns and passes again into the hallway.

And then I might pour myself a cup of tea and gaze down into the warmth. The tea is always so faint, such a pale yellow. I look up at the window in time to see a squirrel jumping from a power line to a tree. I look down. Still no one enters the room. And this is what has convinced me finally that I will not be joined for the occasion, no matter how many invitations I find upon platters scattered around the house, no matter how many kettles are whistling, no matter how many storms I may witness. Several times I think I hear footsteps proceeding from the hallway, or the stairs, or the swishing of linens, of dresses as they approach for the gathering. But each time I look up, the room is still empty. There is no motion in the corridor.

The sleeping figure appears and disappears, and only sometimes do I catch a glimpse of her enough to think that I've recognized her for certain. But other times in her room I am sure that she has just exited. The crumpled bedding, the candle still smoking. Her pen lying on top of the desk and the pile of letters which grows. The letters she writes when I am away are always sealed, the envelope surfaces remain blank.

And sometimes as I am walking up the stairs I think I hear sounds from behind the other doors, which remain locked. At other times I'm convinced that there are not any other guests. But oddly, the teapot does appear empty by the time I return to the sitting room in the evenings.

It may be the thickness of the wavy glass which distorts my gaze, the slightly tilted floors, the drafts which seem to come from nowhere, the road leading to the house, upon which no wheel or foot ever appears.

The humming of the banister, or the gaze of a portrait, or the winking of the red clock seem to hold hidden gestures which I'm at a loss to interpret. And the russet woman in the kitchen, who always disappears before the tea will say nothing, but to remark upon the coming storms. She arrives and departs through a door I've not yet located, upon a path she mentions, behind in the woods, which I've never seen. The history of the house is repeated daily, though not upon any schedule. I feel welcomed in such an odd circumstance, as if by a hostess who has prepared for a large gathering and is only met with one visitor. Or as if I am the hostess, since no one else appears. Then I might laugh out loud, look down into my pale hands and wonder in desperation where the road in front of the house might lead, or if the sleeping figure might ever wake within my presence, and end the fitful sleep of all of the guests which causes the red clock to fly, and the tea to appear faint, and the storms to descend, and the roads to circle the house, never pausing.

S TATEMENT P REPARED BY T HE C HORUS

12 February 2001
Capital Letters Center for Photographic Arts
Post Boxes Rung A—Suite ¡™£¢8
Art Capital, Primary Tributary
CONFIDENTIAL ROUTES

To the Curators of the Permanent Collection
Capital Letters Center for Photographic Arts:

We write to the Capital Letters Center for Photographic Arts regarding a matter so distasteful, that it is with great reluctance that we embark at all. We express regret, and apologize in advance for being the messengers of such a deplorable occurrence.

It has been brought to our attention that someone has been impersonating Ms. Amela, a young woman, whose identity and purposes we now see reason to scrutinize. It has been noted by several of us, that many of Ms. Amela's invaluable prints, the titles of which we cannot presently recall, have been circulating outside of the ordinary channels, no doubt, leaving them open to all the dangers of deterioration and decay which may befall those works which move beyond the sound precepts of archival circumstances. To our knowledge, since Ms. Amela's official death, the estate has been in the sole possession of Marion Clare Cinder, and James Alexander Amela, with the exception of the pieces in your gallery.

It is our hope that you may be able to shed some necessary illumination upon this unpleasant finding and to retrieve the photographs in question. The impersonator at this time is not to be found. The prints in question were last seen in the possession of an Amelia —, who may be implicated in the plot of the impersonator, though we cannot be certain. Unfortunately, at this time we are unable to recall her complete name.

Please disclose the contents of this letter to no one as, of course, you will comprehend, that we don't wish our names to be associated. We trust that you will proceed with caution, and that you understand we have no further intelligence to offer, unless of course you might see fit to seek our services in a discreet manner, and would be prepared to extend some encouragement which might assist us in recalling further trivialities. Assuredly, we hold no expectation for this small disclosure. It is largely our history of successful collaboration with Capital Letters, in our shared interest of preserving art and exhibition spaces for public benefit that we approach you with this difficult news. The security of the collections under your care concern all, and you are no doubt aware that it is often individuals who must bear the responsibility of keeping works in their rightful conditions and locations. We appreciate your confidentiality, as we here saw fit to inform you of this most pressing matter. Please be informed, that having taken the customary security precautions, this letter does not exist in our central data unit, was not sent through the federal postal routes, and will dematerialize within twenty-four hours of your perusal.

Respectfully,
The Chorus

In order to touch speech, I take two decibels back, step upon and water a participle, then hold out my hands which have been scored.

Another aspect of the labyrinth? I seem to be disappearing as well. I walk among the participles of a street dismantled. The photographs begin to breathe. They try to gather me up in their glossy dimensions.

A corridor of time where I would then be clasped, unable to return.

o

In order to touch thought, I order a shroud. I wear my gloved fingertips. I look at nothing directly, but through this small shard of tinted glass.

Once it appeared that the floor tilted in waves. I sought a place where all would not ripple around me. But now the floors tilt naturally. Pens roll off of all seemingly flat surfaces. Landscapes are all susceptible to the same lull. The corners of the room have expanded. Darkness reaches from four directions, until it reaches my center exactly, and covers my eyes with unfamiliar palms.

o

In order to touch sound I seek the heartbeat of a small rat. The cadence of a radiator. I borrow a stethoscope from a cold metal table. I place it against the walls.

The corners of the room fill the entire length and breadth now. I could draw it for you. The angles persist and widen. Unhinging in sharp triangles. In those persistent shadows.

o

In order to touch silence I memorize several sheets of orchestrated quiet. I sit down and do not move. I breathe.

I must have believed once that all time fell into an order that could be counted, and that I knew my place among the numbers. I dropped my weight onto an appropriate page. And waited. I once believed that grounds were relatively straight, that I could walk from one location to the next, and map the places I had been. I have now been adequately reminded otherwise. Expanding corners place and replace me.

In order to record my memories I attempt to depart from the present tense. What awaits me is nonetheless still present.

Where the present drops away. A scaffolding. She led me to this for some reason. I see the edge of my understanding, a small note carried by wind, and over.

I recognize dimly the faint rain, the bare columns of light, my form etched here, pausing in a doorway. But to follow the days and the light, to follow the smallest slips of possible traces.

It is difficult to disbelieve an image in black and white. But that she might have been anyone else.

I disagree with a small shard of tinted glass.

o

In order to touch direct light, I slowly turn my face away from the departing present.

She appeared and disappeared for a reason, unveiled one dimension of the dark, placed me in front of myself. I can describe only where my understanding drops away, the darkness expands, and I walk into it, disappearing from what I once knew. She had been solid once. And now she has entered the ether. If I wish to follow her example I may well be drowned.

o

I disagree with an image in black and white. I find this most perplexing as I wait within a corridor, a faint rain falling upon a slip of darkness. To disagree is also to walk forward, since one must greet the image in order to disagree. I am walking towards the moving image, where it beckons me, into the unfolding darkness.

o

I've arrived at the destination of alphabets, and walk among them. The characters take flight, in an array of beveled edges, and rearrange themselves here in mock sculptures. There isn't any particular order in which they begin. I ask, and this is what I am told:

At the level of the character alone one can find the flight of language.

And then the flock lifts again. I sit beneath the tangle of aerial undulations and gather the limitations of speech, constricted by what most would consider meaning.

I gather that what might be said or written can do little to restore gravity to my room.

I have learned that my name has been assigned to me for no particular reason.

o

I turn a corner. Very small. The walls around me rise pale yellow. I am walking within an elaborate garden, which is a form of belonging. Another whose voice falls away, echoing after my own.

There is the sound of each footstep, and then there is the sound of each foot, and then there is the sound of the stone beneath the foot, and the stone beneath that. That is how the stones understand sound. This is how I learned to recognize voices of the stones as I crossed over them, on my way to the reflecting pool. But when I touch the surface, I can no longer hear them.

Nothing is touched without circumstances. I touch the idle mirror. Trace the edges of it's clouds. I touch the air which surrounds me. I touch the empty reflection. I touch the walls rippling with cilia. I bend to smell the stone flowers.

o

I awaken at the place where all images gather. I look up at the horizon which becomes a slightly trembling screen, pale white streaked with softer gray.

The sky has become transparent.

The place where all color gathers. I am assaulted on all sides at first by it's brightness. Then cooler tones emerge. A mirage of softer voices.

o

In order to touch a participle, I step upon water, and hold out my heartbeat.

I am hovering several feet above the surface of mild waters.

The waters below me rustle. I am suddenly some-what cold.

A voice is growing louder, trying to convince me to release my concentration, which is all that suspends me.

o

I begin to feel a weight pressing down upon me. I am in the river and cold. I crawl to the edge and sit, wringing the water out of my hair. I begin walking away from the stream, and with each step, I can remember less and less of that sensation of hovering, until I find it hard to believe I have fallen into the stream.

I find it hard to believe there is a stream at all, since I don't remember the stream's being. In this part of the wood which I know as I know the leaves about my bare knees. It is only my wet body and garments which convince me otherwise.

Otherwise has wetted me. These woods are not frequent, and neither is water. They are the Neither-Frequented woods, through which all passing this way have passed.

o

In order to keep myself from being captured I sit outside of the present tense and attempt to broach a metal table. The table looks up, but it's expression is not at all as I remember. It is as if, another object has been placed in front of me. The metal ceases to speak.

Once I begin to dry off, as the sun is now fairly strong, I no longer doubt I must have lost my way in this Neither-Wood, and come upon a Less-Frequent-Stream with which I had not before become acquainted.

My memory of hovering becomes replaced with a memory of finding an unfound stethoscope in the consultant's office, which I know, but have not had occasion to wear underwater. The voice has vanished also, the voice which has become gravity.

o

In order to stop being bothered, I approach the stethoscope and place it upon the table.

The stethoscope asks if I'd be more comfortable lying down.

No, I answer, without moving my lips.

What is it I've come for, then, the stethoscope asks.

I answer that my memory has been troubling me. I touch the hesitation of the stethoscope. It ripples.

Present tense? the stethoscope asks. Won't you please rest?

No, it isn't the present tense, I explain. Only the past. Only the past? Is that the entire circumstance?

I know it is not. Since the past seems to swim within the present and the present very clearly points towards the future.

Is that the entire complaint? the stethoscope demands once again.

I remind myself that this particular frame is beginning to melt. The stethoscope looks heavy. The cold metal table begins to blister. I remind myself that I have chosen not to wait upon the table.

I remind myself that the stethoscope can be given back.

I give the stethoscope back.

I walk back across the water. I paint over the metal table. I set aside one cadence of the frame only to document what has happened.

I hear the voice of the radiator. The pressing of the walls. I step into that frame with my circumstances, and drape them over the hooks on the back of my door.

3 MARCH 2001

To The Chorus:

Thank you for your letter of February the twelfth. We appreciate your confidentiality and willingness to participate in the safekeeping of invaluable works of art.

To aid us in our investigation please supply the complete name of Amelia _____, and the titles of pieces in question which you claim to have seen in her possession. We are willing to compensate for this information within the range of code A transfers. Please reply promptly. Customary security precautions (C. S. A.) apply.

Sincerely,
Curators, Capital Letters Center For Photographic Arts
(C. C. L. C. P. A.)

When the corridor was tipped to one side Amelia suddenly saw that it was not at all the hallway she had imagined, but instead a ladder. She saw to it's very top, a bird perched upon what appeared to be a kite. And a flower, upon the head of the bird, with four red petals, distinctly covered in rain. But she hadn't seen the flower until she had almost neared the top. And then she realized that the flower all along had been her voice. She had been speaking all of this time, in four different voices, and each petal represented a different direction. She knew now that she had become very small and light, able to detach herself from her body. With the aid of the ladder she could ascend and descend along the lines of these four petals. But it was a very unusual sort of ladder, the kind upon which it is impossible to tell whether one is traveling up or traveling down. Realizing this, she reminded herself, and the bird agreed, that these terms must remain relative. If earth and sky would not remain still quite long enough for her to determine in which direction she was proceeding, could the difference be of much consequence?

When the corridor vanished completely, and she traveled what seemed a great distance, she had the impression that the first vein of this flower led to a neighborhood where Clara once dwelt. The city contained numerous nuclei, so it wasn't unlikely that one could step several blocks in any direction and suddenly become a stranger within an entirely new terrain. Amelia did this, stepped sideways and downstream and came alongside. The stone streets intersecting at odd five-way bypasses, filtered by wind and soot held a seemingly endless memory. There were signs of distress strewn across her path. She felt herself following marked footsteps down alleyways and avenues. There was the park, which appeared in waves. There were the buildings covered in shadow, and broken shards of glass. And if this were not enough, there were often voices guiding her along. She kept her ear pressed closely to countless parchment thin walls in order to accumulate an array of the faintest conjectures regarding Clara. The streets had not forgotten her. After a time in which quietness enveloped, she finally arrived within the place where nothing could keep silent.

It was said that here, Clara gave dust instead of coins to the homeless upon the many corners. And to this gesture, the recipients said nothing, but met her eye with an understanding which surpassed those who gave quarters. It was said that in the morning, before appearing in front of a glass, her skin was utterly pale. But that the glass warmed her, so that in reflection she appeared brighter than she often was. It was said that she stood still in the park on the coldest days of the year. That she was often seen standing on corners with her purse open.

It was said that she would appear at the dinner hour emerging with a steaming brown paper bag, always the same shape. That she would often walk from one end of the neighborhood to another, without stopping, with no particular errand, that she might pass entire days with this ambling. It was said that she lived in as many as twelve different apartments in one year. She moved about with no possessions beyond a second-hand mattress, a lamp, and a very large and weighty mirror. The mirror seemed an odd choice considering she had no suitcase, no table nor chair, no furnishings whatsoever. She never dined at home, or if she did it was upon the bare floors, with plastic accoutrements. She carried her belongings about in plastic bags. She possessed no coat. Though the winters were not mild, she seemed not to mind them, almost as if she did not notice the ice beneath her feet or the snow covering her arms as so much fleece. She was seen walking barelegged in the snow.

Amelia recognized the mirror from it's description, since many had seen her carrying it through the streets—it had a bold gilt border, in waves and flourishes. There were some inconsistencies in the old glass, which appeared almost as clouds from a distance. Dark splotches upon the surface of lakes. This mirror was the only possession which had accompanied her into her new life. The rest had quietly been drowned when she walked one day into a new series of gestures and streets which soon belonged to her as easily.

Besides the mattress, and the lamp, she had left to the inhabitants of this place of her past existence, a series of exclamations, appearances, and habits which Amelia did not recognize as part of her more recent repertoire. It was said that she was lavish in her fires, in a room in which fires were forbidden. It was said of her that she went everywhere alone, but gazed often across her left shoulder when walking down the street, as if to address a companion. Amelia had the word of more than one that she stopped on several occasions to speak to the man who walked his rabbit down the street on a leash, and the woman with eight dogs who lived in a cardboard box. It was also said, that she always stopped to offer this woman a job. The woman notoriously declined each offer.

On more than one occasion, she was seen covering her eyes with her hands as she entered a particularly dark room. Placing a hand across her mouth as she spoke. Covering her ears in the midst of conversation. It was said that she often smoked more than one cigarette at once. That she slept with her windows open during blizzards. That she was prone to fits of public sobbing. That she owned a telephone, but only made calls from the street. Many claimed to have known her, but none to have known her well. It was said that on more than one occasion, she had fainted, and was seen being escorted home by acquaintances.

25 MARCH 2001.

To C. C. L. C. P. A. :

We are only too happy to supply the information which you request.

However, we believe code C transfer compensation to be appropriate. We realize that you must be as anxious as ourselves to assure the safety of the work in question.

The Chorus

THE LAST PETAL

Amelia despised what had been sent down her throat—tubes, ultimatums, hypotheses standing in the rain, deep shadows which clung as they worked their way down her windpipe, dusk, the murk and the indecision of night, standing in front of a curb in the rain beneath which a lake had gathered, oily black in the street lamps, with small pellets still falling so that she experienced the illusion of vertigo regarding their depths and stepped bewildered with both legs onto the sidewalk and hurried on. The doctor's office was dim and she sat upon a sheet of fresh paper. The day had been a memory of wandering down aisles amid Clara's former closets, of dizzy gowns which appeared towering, stuffed, and dangling by strings. She said nothing of this to the doctor who examined her. Silently she reflected, where do they lead to? If you say nothing when you are asked, you stumble. Rocks parting the way. The gowns hung like dummies, alive and well courted wrapped in plastic. There was apparently nothing wrong with her vision, but still the gowns loomed. The street had lost sight of her. The day had been a catastrophe upon ice. A tattooed lemon, an unstrung shoe, plummeting to it's rightful depths. Then she was lacing her shoes, once all of her clothes had been replaced. She had been making her way down the checkered streets. The day had been many days and the night had been merely hearsay. The construct of dreams colliding with the labyrinth of daily shadows which accompanied her down each tawdry block. The gowns and suits which rose and hung as she walked between them were not merely that, but robes, and avenues and shirt sleeves, and denim slashed and worn, all absent of wearers. All absent of mind. She thought this a bit odd, but the dim office had disappeared. The tide of the garments swept over her, and she continued along, somewhat drenched with apprehension.

THE LETTER "L"

All that was left of her. A few scratches here across a wooden floor, where her chair slid close to her table. The green bottle, and the small black portfolio. The composition notebook filled with lavender, and bergamot. All of the other letters had fled.

Her mistake which was also hers. Which was also the mistake of the century. She spoke to the photographs and asked that they not abandon her entirely. She spoke to the barred windows, and the daybed, and the clock. She tilted her head against the pillow, against the wall, against her own reflection.

The letter "L" surrounded her. She clung to it's sharp angle, gathered it's loll. Placed it below the small of her back, and remembered. The letter which constitutes one gate to an alphabet, one luminous flight, one trick which allowed her to land.

5 APRIL 2001

Chorus:

Unfortunately, C transfer compensation would be impossible. Please reconsider A transfer compensation, which is customary.

C. C. L. C. P. A.

THE CORNERS OF THE ROOM

She begins with the only clues she has: the green bottle, the photographs, the composition notebook. Sebastion. In all of this Sebastion has been present, but she has not seen him entirely.

"Where have I been?" She is sitting in a chair. It is dusk. Her gaze is full upon him.

He senses she has passed through a portal which returns her to the present. He is able to answer honestly. He is less afraid for her now. "Folded into the corners of the room."

"And Clara?"

He is aware that her gaze shifts slightly, when she mentions the name. Her gaze veers almost shyly. He isn't sure how much she remembers—this changes. "Clara has gone away."

"Yes," Amelia assents quickly. Then slowly lowers her head while she asks, "you believe she is dead?"

"No."

"That she has been dead for years?"

"No."

"What then—?"

Still the prodding—he realizes now that she remembers the extent of things and will persist in knowing. But this is what frightens him. That she will persist to search for an answer which may not exist. "That was someone else," he pauses, as if measuring the effects of his syllables, "another Clara" he offers. "Does it matter really which she was? Which was her actual name?" He sees the futility of his statement as soon as it is uttered.

Her reply seems almost involuntary, as he expects. "Yes, it matters terribly." Her gaze falls.

"You know who she is." His tone rises slightly. He is not eager to watch her plough right into the crux which has once been her undoing. But she does not see his concern, only his discouragement.

"I have no idea."

"But you knew her," he continues on, as if to convince her. He begins to see the hopelessness of his task.

"She was as I was."

"Yes," he gives in.

The phrase echoes within her. She was as I was. She was as I was. The only clues in the corners of the room. She dares not reach towards them. "Who was she Sebastion? Who was she?"

"I believe you've had a visitation."

"A visitation from—from where?"

His thought interrupts her own. "From somewhere we cannot fathom."

"What could have been her reasons for lying?"

"If I knew I wouldn't hesitate to tell you."

"I will know—eventually."

"Only—." he says this pleadingly, then breaks off, as if he does not know how exactly to proceed. He gazes at her, in a manner which speaks imploringly.

"I know you want to warn me." she says.

This must be enough, he thinks.

She looks up again, very directly and offers, "I've completed my visit with the corners of the room."

CLARA

And now that she has arisen, to what tasks shall I place her?

I give her this grace, these hands of tapered form. This body somewhat birdlike. This ability to hover. I give her history. I animate her form.

Now she becomes angry with me, when once if I were to vanish, as if the opposite had been true, as if I had been her illusory guide to a landscape at once enchanted and furthermore flawed with the difficulties of non-existence.

Therefore let her seek her own garden. I have imagined her form. She appeared almost as if spun from light.

I was surprised to see her again at the reflecting pool. She did not seem to notice any persons, but to reside as if she were the only person present. And also, as if she were perambulating the edges of a garden within her sole possession.

She speaks not to me but towards my absence, to which I cannot respond.

I correspond with these silences as with the absence of a train which has already departed.

15 APRIL 2001

C. C. L. C. P. A. :

We are beginning to forget the information you require. Your C. S. P. although thorough, place us at some risk. Code B transfer compensation will be acceptable. Complete the transmission, and we will forward the information quickly.

The Chorus

AMELIA

However I sat within the rose garden and played chess with a pheasant or a squirrel. I was disturbed by the sound of a tractor. I was disturbed by the evenly lovely day, and what lay before me perhaps which looked like a garden, and I, a lady of leisure. I was disturbed by the view of the city in the distance, and that none of this really existed. The last time I sat by this reflecting pool the gazebo was already occupied. The lavender visited by bees. A humble aside became perhaps a humble abode. Steps have been traced or reassured. Acres of land whose eyesight have pondered the imponderable pawn.

I supposed that I was mistress of circumstances and only mildly wrought of the temporality of elements which passes between these time strewn hands.

A squirrel became suddenly a tantrum. A humble pawn, perhaps a humble disturbance. And so to hush. I smelled every single rose in the garden, and then went and perched upon a wooden bench. As if anyone could find rest amidst daylight. As if a daylily had nowhere to be. We supply the last rung of the menagerie. I spell and hear the piano, or the weight of the piano. I visit the statuary and make a friend of a large woman of concrete.

Perhaps I will go home now. Perhaps I am approaching my age. Perhaps it is the length of my fingers which makes this thought facile. Perhaps the garden is none of that. A mobile. Nothing is stiff. Do I hunger? Am I exhausted? I wish to walk nowhere, but the body will be mobile. Song persists. No visitors approach finely. And otherwise I, a pilgrim, will persist and travel nowhere widely. The sky interacting. Nothing is white. The weight of a piano or daylily of concrete. Nothing else. No less orchestrated sky.

I'd like to say something much more benevolent. To press against the moment where thirst is an accomplice. I trust the deep gravity of a gaze, the mildness of the weather or the intuited echo of the body's motion. I lament at having a form which seems remote. But if all were immediate would longing persist?

5 MAY 2001

Chorus:

After careful review we have concluded that our collections show no missing pieces. Our investigation is complete. We withdraw our request for information.

C. C. L. P. A.

125

PART THREE:
BOOK OF GOSSAMER AND LIGHT

i.

A Photograph in Black and White

"It is one thing to insert yourself into a mirror, but quite another to get your image out again and have your errors pass for objectivity."
—Rosmarie Waldrop

Walking down wetted streets the slight illumination passing lights falling upon the sidewalk which she imagined had never before appeared black.

He began measuring words to their walk. Of this she heard little at first, and seemed to enter in only when she noted a shift which she imagined as the switch from a blunt to a sharp instrument.

He had said, "The problem is not who matters terribly, but who does not." He watched her looking down at the pavement as they walked. There was no doubt that the question had been antagonistic, but it seemed to take this for her to begin.

That was, she imagined, the night's alchemy. His insistence upon difficult speech. She paused, "In such small dimensions you describe—." She had not looked up.

"Describe?"

A dark palate inset with a variable shimmer disappeared in shadow and seemed to crawl or tumble along. The cold on her spine, the sound of gravel filled steps.

"How else then does the world descend and exist for you?" he persisted not at all unaware that her steps were also inset with uncertainty which carried her, reluctantly at first outside of the warm interior of a rented room.

Out reluctantly past the dip in the road where the trees moved in and darkness no longer visited but surrounded. Reluctantly past the bridge over the ravine, and the brighted windows, whose lives were ever curious as the one which walked alongside her, resisting the temptation to look up, into those which could not be anything but complete, when beheld from a distance. "Will you taunt me then, with the shadow of that boisterous chorus?" It was their affectionate, though derogatory classification of those persons who appeared to them to proceed flatly along the scenery. And yet they knew this to be unfair. Simply talk. Another flat way of seeing.

His answer was prompt, "Yes."

She had almost forgotten him, though he held the umbrella in one arm and his other was wrapped around her securely. She had forgotten falling into step. It wasn't forgetfulness exactly, but as if his movements had become extensions of her own. His speech a mechanism of her listening. His walk the rhythm of her thought. "Simply put, I exist for them not any further then they for myself."

At this he balked at the seeming untruthfulness of her statement. She had seen directly through the veneer of concentrated talk, but had missed that true concern within which it swam, within which she had not been overlooked. He was convinced that though she had tossed aside the depths of her distress, she still should look further around, and not mistaking the once slate gray overhead which had now become a rough screen surrounding her. "You interchange them as if they could be reassembled." He wanted her to allow others to exist for her again. And why not begin easily, with the known, those who were familiar. He said, "You disregard all consideration. Yet you are at the center of concern."

She continued, reluctantly beyond the shadow of her spine, the dark crawling of a bridge over the cold interior, brightened by the one who walked beside her. "It is not 'I' at the center of their talk, but more likely, someone who resembles me little."

He shivered as if the umbrella securely overhead had fallen. The trees pushed closer.

"The only difference" she went on "is that she exists much more convincingly."

The road narrowed, rubbed against the sides of their legs, streaked across the thin canopy, spoke from above to their senses, dropped their ornaments of water.

"The world beyond this doubling may be wider than you imagine." He thought, the bridge would do well to look past the shadow.

"I have to warn you," she hesitated. Her gaze was still fixed below. "It matters terribly that I am not she." She was studying the alchemy of the shadow, whose lives were ever so curious, not anything but complete, when narrowed within the imagined palette, inset with precise light.

He failed to capture the vision. "You've done your best to assert just the opposite."

It was as if they no longer visited this street, but had added the precise light with their steps, which shook off of the trees and made actual their wandering. "I assure you," she said, finally looking up, and falling out of step as she did so, "I've done all I can to pull my reflection from hers."

The darkness maintained a certain viscosity, through which resistance had been necessary to begin. But now that they had begun, they continued. Without the question of turning back.

AMELIA

All is correspondence. My very lip in motion speaks to you. Nothing other than that. Who obliges this labyrinth to open.

I couldn't find this in a book, the place where presence vanished. No one had warned me about the curious opposition of a squirrel falling out of a tree. Standing in snow perfectly still while the downtown crowds prod and rush.

I tempted the white skies. Where to—?

This is what you will experience next. The determined rolling down a hill.

How to speak, how to walk. How to fill that interminable moment of doubt when one appears or disappears.

She couldn't find this in the landscape surrounding her. The eyes which were not her eyes.

A torch remains outside my window, because one day it will not.

It will not proceed that the cloud cover is less blue today, more marvelously soft upon the hills of shoulders in the distance.

Loss has been constructed. It can not be found on the surface of water.

I have been watching bodies contrary to the daily light.

Her words remember for me and I watch as the hill recants.

It is my vision which persists.

There are damsels drowning in a lake, whose blue faces—.

Their bodies supply ink, wine, vantage points. At which I am posted.

She is still opposable.

Emerged perhaps from a rose to discard the landscape about her, only because everything was too large. She befriended a swallow.

Yet I was not a swallow.

Or perhaps with precision, she took refuge in the rose.

C ONSTRUCTIONS

They sit, with Amelia's notebooks open across their laps, Sebastion marveling at the detail.

"You don't see? Already you have trespassed." He insists.

Amelia does not answer for a moment. "Yes," she pauses, "though you speak as if I were not fluent."

"Much to my fright—I almost wish you had not been!" He turns his head with emphasis. "But that is foolish of me."

"It has been incredibly useful actually. And you might have had no idea where I had been, if I had not made an attempt to record everything."

"I am glad," he assents, but then continues stressing his speech, "I don't wish to worry you needlessly, but precautions still are necessary."

"Precautions?"

"We should not revisit too often, at least, not in the near future—" he falters, "what I mean to say is, I wouldn't think it wise for you to revisit these notes alone, at least for the time being." He has said it and now he imagines he has made both of them uncomfortable.

She seems slightly amused at this notion of his fear, as if it were unfounded. "Would you have me not recount?" She realizes that the question isn't entirely a fair one, but she wants to know what he will do with it.

"Your memory—" he considers then pauses. "There are other passages to revisit."

"Shall this one be the locked tower then? From which I will be denied entrance? But you forget," she says, holding her arms open and standing still as if to demonstrate, "It is not possible to keep me out of it." She closes one notebook after another, and piles them in a stack upon the table within reach. " You are right, I don't need to read them, but that is hardly a precaution."

The notebooks are every color. Gold piled upon blue. Yellow upon crimson.

But she hasn't finished, "You are reading them now, aren't you? For your own amusement? "

He is still studying her earlier question. "I only meant, you ought not to be going over and over—"

"Yes," she considers, "as a precaution, you mean that I might choose a transparent subject?"

"If you can find one." He seems relieved at her ability to see through his meanderings. To pick up a thread of intercourse which once baffled her.

She goes on. "That would be your story, the one that you tell yourself. That is all." She restacks the notebooks—green upon violet. "They are no more than stories" she promises, turning around slowly to reach him. "That is the story you tell yourself, that I must not remember, that it might be dangerous. But I remember it perfectly. This is your story. I merely exist within it. You are the one telling it. I am perfectly through." She steps away now from the table supporting the evidence as if to demonstrate her point.

He realizes the fault of his reasoning. Sees that she is beyond him and yet she has always been, as one autonomous being is always beyond the reach of another. He thinks, I have done what I can for her. I am at best, imperfect. But he says only, "I understand."

All of the notebooks are closed one by one. The story of transparency ends here.

Snow

She said that the book had once seemed larger to her, the hardback white covered book had seemed perhaps twice the size in recollection because when she had first come across it, she had been within a much smaller apartment. Thus all objects in the room had taken upon themselves larger dimensions, as the walls shrunk around them, which were in any case more like curtains as they seemed to flutter, but still remained walls in their ability to push one further. They had come to this realization while sitting by the fire. He holding her gaze as if he were to prevent her from falling within an abyss which might lie, she supposed, vaguely past the ends of their toes. It was somewhere beyond their toes, and beside the hearth. It was unmistakably within the room, but then nowhere to be seen. She did not admit to the abyss. The admission of the size of the book was enough. His gaze was certain to keep her well away from it's brink, even without the sight of it. His arms carried her within what seemed a safe distance. This room, unlike the apartment which originally contained the book when her eyes had first fallen upon it and her fingers had first faltered gladly across it's pages, this room had no ability to magnify the objects it contained. This room had the opposite flair, and just as easily transformed the substantial into the smallest presence.

She had become dwarfed. This she could admit, along with the book which once seemed larger, as had her perceptions. She explained this in the afternoon while they walked along in the snow. The unexpected blanket unloosed her lips. She gazed around her at the surprising brightness and found movement which had long since been blotted by the weather. The early dark, the descent of the year and it's baffling new covering which led everything unwittingly along.

They entered a large park now. A child turned abruptly and landed in a heap of powder. Two young men were skiing down the steps. There was no fear in their faces. The square had been covered with snow in the space of a few hours. The cherry trees, which once appeared contracted, in fists and bulges were now softened. She was explaining that in those faces of the young men on the steps, was an attitude she easily recognized. The phrase written invisibly across their faces, muttered endlessly: I will find that, that which I will become. The spirit of endeavor, if only one could subtract arrogance, could be retrieved and possibly put to use. In a number of years the phrase that once muttered proudly across their faces might be dancing madly, I have only so much time. Or, what has any of this amounted to after all ? And then those faces might admit benignly to the impossibility of the dimensions originally imagined. And resort once again to falling into the powder.

This was precisely what happened to the white book, which once seemed so grand in scale, and later became the book that it was. This book which impressed her still, she held in her lap as night fell upon the square and the cherry trees so many blocks away. The child was removed from the powder and put to bed. The skis abandoned. There the abyss formed between the dinner hour, and the thicker darkness, while the sledding continued outside their windows, and sometime since the fire had caught.

It did not exist during the daylight, or if it did she was not aware of it as any location. Perhaps there were days when it swallowed the entire room, but then she must not have known. The room seemed to invite her. If she could speak of it, it might disappear entirely. If she could speak of it, there would be less of an arrangement with herself not to speak of it, not to grope around it's edges. For this evening, the admission of the book had been enough. The hours passed until eventually the abyss became something lighter, if it in fact did exist. The corners of the room rose to meet her in waves of what seemed warm liquid surrounding her. Escorting her towards that other consciousness where the room contained instead an inviting lagoon. She awoke upon it's edges and took her first steps into the water without fear.

REMNANTS

She imagines the deserted studio. Possesses a key. One lone teacup perched upon a window ledge. Belongings carelessly strewn. It was a miracle she did not trip over such emptiness. She stands looking into a mirror eating an apple. An apple which must be red.

She hears Sebastion's voice from the scaffoldings of the present begging her not to continue.

She steps away from the mirror, and the possessions vanish. She walks across to the wood stove. Touches it. Finds it is cold, gazes out the window once more, finds nothing, and so departs.

SUNDERED LIP

The morning approximately shuffled. And then she didn't wish for anything more. So the wishing and the shuffling stopped and he found it within himself to speak.

She was walking past him in the time of year when streets begin to shift. She once would have followed his eye, but stopped, since his had never caught.

Though he had not grown any bolder, some mechanism within him was lifted, brought about by his desire to solve. He saw her recovery as a puzzle and held that he could contribute to it's completion. He had always been good with puzzles, and he considered that although she treated him badly, since she was unwell, it would be incorrect to withhold. He could not bear the thought of being incorrect. He held that he never had been incorrect before.

He imagined that others knew that he might know something, but on this count he was mistaken. And so his motivation to be recognized as correct would not be realized, but in seeking her out, this was his original design. He did think it somewhat odd, somewhat ill fated that she who had tampered with his destiny should assist hers in a manner so benevolent. Speech was the object with which he imagined himself heavily carrying a correct obligation. Nothing more.

When her eye did not catch his, he paused, and in doing so nearly collided with her, whose steps were directed deliberately downward, and only faintly registered his. She had become accustomed to this manner of travel and had learned that persons generally will part ways, and circumambulate around a creature despondent with head bowed. But he did not. She was forced to look up or to broach heads. She looked up, and saw immediately that his gaze was deliberate and that it held something. What it was she could not imagine but she could only guess that after so much avoidance perhaps he had softened, or that possibly now he wished really to look at her. It was true, she noticed, that now that she did not present herself nearly as often she was stared at. She was used to being stared at for other more obvious reasons, which she attributed to her oddness. She did not guess anything otherwise. She knew that all too often eyes fell upon her, and that she would somewhat float in order to avoid attention. She did not know that this ethereal manner, developed somewhat as a defense, as an attempt to remain invisible had exactly the opposite effect. She became a curiosity because of it.

All of this changed when she fell, as some saw it, into a cavernous pit, and agreeably remained with almost no visitors. This was how he saw her, as one emerged only momentarily from the cavern to execute a crucial errand, a dash into the upper worlds. She seemed dressed for such an errand, and her posture suggested as much. He eyed her carefully, as if trying to determine the nature of her quest. She had been innocently walking, which he took as an invitation to interrupt, whatever it might be, to detain her, and to give her a small parcel, a penny of information, if she would allow him. Then he reasoned, he could console himself with the knowledge that had she never known, it would not have been by any fault of his. But how to suggest? It would be too abrupt to inform her of his intention. He did not wish to alarm her. He needed some pretense.

"Which direction are you walking?" he asked, which made her smile slightly since he must be aware, since they had nearly collided, that she was walking in the direction directly opposite to that of his, whichever way that happened to be. But she didn't answer upon the impulse she might have before, since she was surprised at his boldness in stopping her, after such a long lack of contact. Instead she pointed, and he looked at a small grocery on a corner a block away. He noticed a small cafe next to the grocery, and found his excuse.

"Have you had lunch already?"

The hour was barely noon, and although she could see the invitation approaching, she could not bring herself to decline. She nodded that she had not, still aware that she had said nothing.

"Would you join me then?" He paused. This was spoken, they were both aware, in a superficial manner which did not at all fit their previous interactions. But it was spoken with friendliness, and the spontaneity of the invitation pressed her.

"All right," she said. And they began to walk together towards the small cafe. She was also tempted by her former curiosity regarding him. Although she had given up her original designs of collaboration she had never entirely abandoned her interest.

They reached a table and sat. He over a cup of black coffee, and she over a luncheon more complete than she had had this entire month, mostly since she spent much time in solitude, and in such a state she had developed the habit of forgetting her hunger. The conversation was at first awkward, she found, having forgotten also the habit of conversing with all but a few. There was a slight breeze which was surprisingly warm and damp. The street, visible from where they sat seemed all the more animated compared to their quiet corner, suffused with light and warmth. She did not know what to do with all of this. Her hands oddly mechanical. His gaze fell uncomfortably into his lap. But it was only for a certain small number of exhaustingly long moments before he again took up his former tone as if they had been intimate friends separated by inconsequential details of difficult schedules and frequent travel. This was charming, and so she took up the tone where she was instructed to do so by his pauses, relieved to have a prompt of scripted responses. Encouraged by her cooperation he began to skirt around the parcel he wished to suggest. He started by vaguely asking of any news.

"News?" she answered somewhat roughly, to indicate she was unaware of his intent. His polite script had dropped from her fingertips. The awkward silence threatened. He was determined to rescue their meeting.

"I don't mean to pry," he began deciding quickly on another topic, then aware that he had set entirely the wrong tone. Why had he used the word pry? Her expression was falling. "What I mean is, that I wish to inquire as to the state of your health—but not to be intrusive." He seemed pleased with himself now. This was easy enough.

"My health?" she answered, "my health is very good thank you."

"I'm glad to hear it. We have seen so little of you this season, I feared that you might be unwell."

"Unwell, perhaps, but my health is. . " she paused, unable to disallow the subject entirely, "I'm sufficiently recovered," she smiled. "Of course, you know that I've suffered quite a shock."

"Yes, of course," he assented. "I'm sorry. You refer to the disappearance of your friend?"

She guessed by his features that this was the subject he originally meant to broach.

"Forgive me for being so direct," he went on, "but I've not been clearly informed. And I wondered if there were anything I could do to help, that is, if you'd allow it." Once again, now that he had spoken he was impressed with how easy it finally had been. He watched her face carefully as her expression hesitated, and a reluctant control fell over her features.

"It was that more or less," she said, "but. .," she hesitated, then met his gaze, as if to challenge the statement. "Her identity," she faltered, "all—even that is still unclear."

"Yes, I think I understand." He drew his features together in sympathy. "I'm sorry. Forgive me for bringing up so difficult a subject." He paused, and then continued, more tentatively. "I do have reason to do so."

This alarmed her. She sat up in her seat and she tossed down the scripted niceties. Her hands regained their confidence. She was completely within her senses, and he could see that all trace of her former reluctance, the last remnants of her lapses had vanished. He remembered her now as she was, and his anger returned, but he pushed it aside. He was determined to follow through with his intention.

"Let me explain." He paused. "I was hoping that I might help you to solve the question which troubles you."

She lifted her gaze, which had become defensive. She had not wished to discuss this with him. It was like going over old fathoms of gathered cloth, and finding all of the imperfections, all of the holes in the work she had constructed. He seemed now to know this. Her curiosity dissolved. A latch had been caught, and there would be no continuing. He stopped. She was polite, but she was annoyed. She assumed that his reasons for 'bringing it up' were to demonstrate his wish to come to her assistance, when of course there was nothing that he could do. She was now for him someone to be examined, consoled. Simply another scripted measure he misconstrued.

He saw it was no good. He would not succeed today. He thought he had been prepared, but he had not. He should have known better than to try, like this, a chance meeting. It was too much. He turned the conversation to himself, his work slowly. She resumed the appropriate scriptedness and they able to get through the occasion There was no reference to her previous involvement in this. She spoke as if it were all new to her. He described the turn his work had taken, since he had rejoined the syntactical assemblage of the dimly concentrated tables. And when they had exhausted their conversation and appetites they awkwardly stood in the doorway briefly, and he took her hand and said, "I'm very glad to see that you are well, and hope that I will be seeing more of you." She was remembering her errand now, her retreat and her abode, and the rest of the day stretched before her, momentous in it's dimensions.

"Thank you," she said.

———————————

She supposed all things being unequal, that she had been led to an eclipse. A leaping off point. She was either present, or she was not. He either had some information or offered her nothing. But this type of explanation was of no use to her now. The "she" which exited out of this discernible frame might as well have been one aspect lost. She supposed there was a piece of this mosaic missing. She supposed and then frowned upon the scenery around her. Her closet of vagaries was growing. She found herself suddenly again without resources. She had earlier imagined herself as blessed with innumerable supports, buttresses of fashionable lengths and styles. Arches held up by delight alone. The newness of each day had been enough. The light fell upon her face as if it had found her. Had she known that this unexpected meeting would throw her carefully recovered balance askew, she would have more often looked up and bathed her features in the glow of the mid afternoon. Steps in subtle traceries of streets had once again been neatly combed and set in front of her in intricate designs. Elaborate patterns of asphalt and stone. Cement staircases and wooden landings. She knew not where to begin, and spent the entire afternoon wandering aimlessly amid the possibilities which might have been imparted.

She Rearranges the Ghost

All of her letters must permit a trace. A series of permutations, which when placed in one possible formation, may determine her whereabouts.

Clara Amela. Clear lace. Ell reel. Lamela camera. Amell. Lac, a lame mare. Err call acre. Race era. Ream marl. A clean cell. Allar care ale. Marcela cream. Mace ear. Arrear area. Cram alee. A calm raceme. Leer meal. La rare mal.

Alar arm. Lamé elm arc. Mammal lees. Alma. Calla carrel. Me—ere, a la lam.

Amelia

Though she had supposed the winter to be forgotten, the snow began to fall and continued to blanket her thoughts. Into evening, heavily, until looking out not a speck of the gray street was visible. Piled into monuments of white.

The following day she combed the streets. She stood beside the hidden river. She walked below the gleaming edges of rising glass. All along the boulevards huge piles of snow plowed into miniature glaciers, advancing above the tops of cars and small trees, barricading the entrances to shops. The abrupt sides of vast crushed ice were before her, a sheer wall of icicles overhung her. The solemn rushing of traffic was broken only by brawling dogs on leather leashes, the scuffling of some uncertain shoe, the underground trains, and the cracking which reverberated along the curbs of accumulated ice, rent and torn turning darker every hour. What had once been a pristine sea of white perfectly described. Where once she had been subdued she could no longer retire to rest. Her slumber had been in vain. She awoke to find a scene far more dismal than that which she had left the evening before.

We rest; a dream has power to poison sleep.

We sleep; poison rest to a power, dream has.

In the morning she found this whispering powder. From above the pristine white was tenanted. From this vantage point, she rediscovered the spectrum.

She followed the stairs which led to the roof. A mist covered the streets below. The surface was uneven, rising and buckling.

A boiling black sea.

In this cold?

Yes, it once boiled, and now here it rises. Here it rises. Where she stood now the skyline directly opposite. Though she had awakened with a complete sorrow, the buildings wrapped in cloud could carry a silent plea.

She thinks, if you are present, why do you allow me this faint recognition only of your once constant self?

If I were present?
There is only white, a boiling black sea.
Not a speck of color?
Only white
Find the color in this picture.

Suddenly she did see a branch emerging as a denser shade of dust. A cloud much too heavy to be called white. She stepped carefully back over the buckling bridges, the boiling soot, down the crumbling staircase. The yellowing crumbling staircase. The peeling blue of the hallway. The dim yellow of a bare bulb. The once green of the fading carpeting. Back to her window edged in lavender. The street below closer now.

Find the color in this picture.

The lamppost sleet. The small tips of trees where snow had begun to clump and fall away, a tentative green-gray. A passing coat, vivid red, the child within, almost no skin apparent. The paler lips. The black mittened hands and burgundy cap. An auburn braid tossed from shoulder to shoulder as she skidded, quite deliberately from patch to patch of ice.

FROM PATCH TO PATCH OF ICE

As white skies became smudges and trees silhouettes. A voice lilting across water. There was a knock at the door, or so she thought. As soon as she opened it the day opened upon the cold cement. As soon as she opened the door, mist again. Approaching the subway, a dense fog of suspended ice particles. Descending, she thought without measure, each column of steps. Then standing amidst that palpable sea, held up only by clutching the metal pole. Bracing. The opening doors. Osmosis.

She stands in the half dark on the other side of the waiting tracks. A shadow crosses. Scent of bergamot. Battered suitcase. On the other side she sees what appears actual. She sees a back turned and walking swiftly in the other direction. The hem of a coat brushing ankles. She sees a black buttoned waist, which twists to look into the racing light.

The train is approaching. She calls. Across the tracks. Nobody seems to hear, to notice. The coat, the suitcase and their possessor board the train which disappears into the tunnel.

THE SHADOW GUEST

Clara is sitting on the train, scribbling in a notebook, her suitcase on the seat across from her.

Conversing with what is not actual, Amelia boards.

Possibly there is no train. This seems to make little difference.

She moves over the suitcase. Sits across from Clara. Folds her hands. Clara looks up. Looks down again to the page. Full of black smudges.

"Clara?"

She looks up only vaguely. Amelia unfolds her hands. Again, repeats her name only.

"Clara?"

Clara is listening to the light. She draws a circle with her eye upon the clouded window-glass. She shifts her gaze to the seat across from her. She looks up, disbelieving.

Amelia considers. She desires a singular speech of the present, not a tracing of the peripheries of what has passed. She lapses for a moment. Then she stands and crosses over, sitting beside her. She waits to be met.

Clara shifts her focus. She looks out the window of the train, through her imaginary circle on the glass. Gazes at the fog, moving in thickets. "How did you find me?"

Amelia pauses. She has not considered this question. "It was by chance," she finally replies and as she speaks she notes a proclivity approaching—Clara's expression floats.

"It was not by chance. You followed me."

Amelia watches her detach as she speaks. The suitcase shifts slightly on the opposite seat. Clara reaches over to steady it, steps across, and remains seated on the other side. She has not imagined this. She thinks, to vanish, and then to have one believe—.

Clara interrupts her thought, "I had you believe? Had you believe—what?"

Clara is listening to her now, but listening as she would listen to the light, to an object. She listens through or despite. Despite, Amelia is determined to continue. "I believed who I thought I once knew."

"And now you disbelieve?"

It is as if she has been practicing. But she does not say this, instead she lapses. "If I were to board a train—."

"If you were to board a train, disentanglement has everything to do with speed, nothing with sight." Clara is beyond listening now. She is seeing as well.

Nothing to do with sight, a difficult clue, she thinks, and replies "I cannot exist there." She thinks of the Neither-Frequented woods, where she did not remain. "You disappeared with no word"

"Magnificent words which no one ever uses."

Amelia muses, there are beasts, and then there are beasts. And none will be captured or explained. "But to vanish?"

"You know how often it happens."

Through which all passing this way have passed, Amelia thinks.

"You've done so yourself," Clara continues.

"Vanished?"

"Yes, in a manner of speaking. Where have you been precisely, since we last met?"

She thinks, I have been inside a large chamber, a pretty box, lined with flowers. I have been walking the perimeters of a precarious shadow. "Since we last met?" she replies, "I could not tell you." Amelia sees the vantage point now from which her companion gazes. But it is from gazing at this distance that she has lost perspective.

"Precisely" Clara replies.

"First you found the distance. I only followed. You must have known." She pauses. "But you have not vanished." Her statement is tentative. This question which has plagued her.

"Not entirely," Clara answers.

"For a reason?"

"I was following you as well. You, who step upon air. You cannot pretend I belong here either." The trail end of a passing storm scrolls beyond the windows. A device has fallen.

Amelia is suddenly cold. "Something pressing?" She begins to feel a weight, further than explanation, beyond that. Beyond cressy and twilight. Beyond their repertoire of accomplished disguises.

"You could say I'm late already."

"Being carried off?"

"The picture moves away. And I within it. It's too ridiculous. You've come to find me out. And I've come to see you off."

"But I am not departing." She wonders, how to find a fitting answer, how to question.

"Departing from the present? All that has passed? A former notion? A similar distinction—truly." Nothing can explain the brightness in her expression as she speaks these words, as if she were giving something away. An extraordinary vision. A point from which to focus.

"Yes, the picture moves away."

I have believed all of it, she thinks, though I have been led away from the moving picture. "And then there is the picture which does not move at all. The picture which we imagine, but which is not actual."

"Such a portrait can move with more facility."

"The difference is whether or not you discriminate between the actual and—" she pauses, uncertain what to call this, this, and settles on, "other."

"And do you, discriminate?"

"I do since you seem to require this of me," she answers somewhat perplexed at her words. They have been drawn from a sentiment she was not yet aware of consciously.

"Have I required you here as well? Do I bring you to everything?" Clara's face looks plain, suddenly flat, with no entrance in terms of her expression.

At this Amelia doubles over a bit. She answers the question in some sense she has not yet explored, a sense which makes her ill to consider. Clara follows her dismal gaze as it drops towards the floor between her feet. She abruptly closes her notebook and Amelia's eyes flutter shut. She pulls it open again absently filling the silence, until Amelia looks up.

"Yes" she finally answers, "you have brought me to this." She feels as if her sight is growing dim. As if her power of thought has been wrenched away from her, and returned somewhat distorted.

"It's impossible to explain. I can tell you only what I see." She studies the figure inhabiting the dress. "But you mustn't follow the frame. It's impossible to follow." She is listening with her eyes once again to an object. She is silenced by this shadow.

The silence begins once again. It stretches out to fill space surrounding, until she hears only the rattling of distances passing. It fills the somewhat distorted land-scape.

She sits looking out the window at the fingers of mist. The passing verbiage. The past and the passing through which all passing this way have passed. The unmapped premises. She keeps her gaze directed away from the suitcase resting on the otherwise empty seat across from her.

CLARA

She is silenced by a shadow. As if a streamer of form were entirely in her care.

And who she was in relation to the "Clara" who was expected to emerge, as opposed to this other, less lumi-nary character she found herself inhabited by often, she could not foretell. Without so much as one image to claim as her own.

She is silenced by this one who comes to seek her out, who sweeps along her own myth. Bringing with her, her own emptiness and companions.

o

Clara stands up from the stone bench, disentangling her arm from her sister's shoulders. She clasps the black portfolio. The one not noticed to be missing. She steps out of the picture entirely. Leaving merely an impression.

It's impossible to tell, she explains to the dress pinned to her wall. The shadow guest has been late today, and then the light appears, dappled, transparent, elusive as always. A tonic to her senses, this late afternoon.

She had been alone, and then silence commenced speaking with her.

AMELIA AND SEBASTION

So lost had she been in thought that she nearly forgot her promise to meet him. A fifteen minute walk. Her promise walking, she imagined. She looked at her wrist considering, coat billowing behind her. Down the broken stairs briskly, only pausing briefly before her mailbox and pulling out an envelope which she studied uncertainly in the faint buzz of the landing. The hand she did not recognize. Small curls of green upon blue. She had been delinquent in all of her correspondences and was not lately accustomed to small careful pages such as these. She scrutinized the return address with no success. She tore it open, still unable to guess. The pages turning her fingers found the signature of her recent unexpected lunch partner. She crumpled immediately, without thinking. Then pressed out against the glass of the door, folded carefully, and placed a question in her coat pocket, assuming that whatever her hand contained, she would be best off to discover once she had reached him.

Enlivened by the letter, she walked quickly past the iron stair banisters, the waiting corners, counting as she went along the possibilities contained within her hand. She clutched with just as much trepidation as she did pleasure. It had been so long since the outer world had sent her any meaningful signs. It had been long since she had seen or heard her surroundings in such a way which might allow in any subject which deviated from her carefully contained premise of abandonment, that she began to doubt their existence. But as she walked now the outer world rose around her in sinuous arcs. She was determined now to follow the clues she had formerly abandoned. And here her resolve to disclosure wavered. Sebastion's main concern was not to unravel, but to secure. He might doubt any information the letter contained. He might discourage her meeting again with it's author. This new consideration was unsettling as she walked stirring the water which surrounded her with sudden disturbance. She knew she must pursue the questions. This rushing through the street absentmindedly, forgetting the time and her person. She decided silently to say nothing, not even of her chance meeting. There were other things with which to unburden herself. He would suspect nothing from what she was about to confess. He would be in the room with the most sunlight. It would be morning. She would find him in that moment of quietness in which his face would hold an open rhythm, and there possibly she would be able to speak as she had not spoken before.

He sat with his gaze following her footsteps until she too was seated within the small circle of light. Until she was engaged within the quietness, the rhythm created by the table and the curtains drawn open, and the mid morning contemplation. It was a comfort to her to be able to find him. To find her way through familiar streets. To visit his habit of residing within time, to be certain that someone still knew how to do this. Since after all, only he had followed her passage back from corners which had seemed immense. There had been others nearby, before the floors had gone straight again, but not in so many dimensions. There had not yet been an occasion where he had ceased to exist for her entirely. She was grateful for the quietness of his thought which could persuade her to see something in the morning itself.

That was why she had come. To cast down, if just for a moment what came before, and what would come later. There were invitations which she could not give herself. His movements alone could engrave and deliver a message which she herself might have invented.

He greeted her silently.

"How do I find you?" she asked, less sure of his mood in the brightness and stillness than she would have been if they'd been out walking. The day fell somewhat arched across his features.

"The same as every morning, except a bit anxious at what you've uncovered," he answered.

"Uncovered?" she asked, taking up her place to begin, since he was the only one who could accept her subtle offerings.

"You've been dreaming?" he asked.

"Quite possibly you have been," she suggested. This replying to her unspoken thoughts continued to startle her. She felt now less ready to speak.

"What did she say?"

"Who?" She breathed audibly. "Who?" she demanded. The question would give her time.

He was well aware he had overstepped. Still he continued. "Her," he said, as if that made everything plain.

"Her? Tell me plainly then, since you seem to know."

He looked at her slowly. Trying to match his hesitation to her own.

She paused, "I'm not certain it's a dream I've come to discuss. I've come to discuss yesterday."

"Yesterday, how do you mean?" he asked.

"I mean that I was not asleep." She emphasized each word, giving them equal weight, as if so much depended upon her stringing of syllables. As if her meaning might otherwise betray her speech.

"A waking dream?" he asked.

"A euphemism between us of late—" she answered. "I won't argue any further. I saw her yesterday."

He was determined not to lose his composure. Not to betray his speech. As he stood upon a disintegrating hillside. "Where?" he asked stumbling.

"I was waiting for a train." She paused. She saw him now trying to enter the picture. She was determined though to describe it as it had been to her waking sense. "She was on the other side," she continued, "with her back to me. She was boarding. She didn't hear. The strangest thing was, that nobody seemed to hear." She thought, as often nobody seems to hear. The silence surrounded them for an instant.

"Or perhaps, pretended not to hear?" he said, "Were you certain it was her?"

She did not answer this. "I got onto the train and spoke with her."

"You were on the other side of the tracks?"

"Yes."

"So you must have moved very quickly if she was boarding when you first saw her." He was going over all of this, imagining the steps she might have taken.

"I remember boarding" she said.

He paused at this. Wasn't going to approach any sort of explanation. "How was she?" he asked oddly, aware of the awkward sound of the question.

She began to pace while clutching her pocket. As if walking around an imaginary object, he thought.

"She spoke around herself. Around me." And then she thought, it was much like the conversations I have with myself.

"In what way—?" He was aware now that she had lost the strain of his presence.

"She explained nothing." The frustration was audible in her pitch.

"Did you ask her—?" He said, as if he had been with her then. He tried to drop all doubt.

She looked down. "She explained, but only in ways which make sense from within the frame. Do you see? You must see."

She seemed to see him again for an instant and so he continued his absurd questions. He wasn't sure why. "What did she say?"

She did not hesitate at this. "She said she'd come to see me off."

This startled him. "Where are you off to?" he asked.

"Exactly nowhere, I assure you" she answered.

"Are you certain of that? Perhaps you know. Have you considered?" his gaze implored her to stand still, to focus.

"It seemed to me like a manner of saying good-bye."

He released his breath. Sat heavily in relief. He had been waiting for a similar scene to present itself, and now finally recognizing the occasion, he rushed towards it, while simultaneously trying to disguise his running. He held his features in place and said, "Nothing more natural." Then he laughed, "Very much like her."

She hadn't fathomed the humor. "I felt physically ill, as if I had been struck. And that was close to the end of it."

"The end of it"? he questioned. But she seemed not to notice so he did not press. He shifted his tone "And how do you feel now?"

"Better," she looked up again, finally. "As if the dream has ended," she caught herself saying. "But it wasn't a dream," she insisted, seeing the tangle she had created.

"It makes little difference really" he said.

She knew that a dream was no less true. They agreed upon that point. But it was his next observation, the one that nearly escaped her, which caught her up and buried her breath for an instant. He paused. "Don't you see?

"What is it?" she asked, and it struck her then, heavily, numbly, and his words echoed her thoughts precisely.

"She has finally released you," he said.

It was Sebastion's art to go to the center of a thing without touching it. If he could have dissuaded her he would have done so. If he could have stepped into the dream he wouldn't have hesitated. He would not have waited for her to appear, mid-day, flustered. He would have followed her now, if she'd shown him the passage.

And yet the question of Clara's identity held little interest for him. Clara had delicately faded and Amelia had reappeared. Clara was a passing forgetfulness. He had sat with her, walked by her side, attended her parties, dined upon her conversation. Once she'd been terribly present. The rest had fallen out of focus. He'd never bothered to ask where she had appeared from. She was false. A false friend disappears. It needn't matter why. But what had been the nature of her relationship with Amelia? What had Clara wanted of her? There had been a lingering discomfort about her—in her magnetic adagios. The way she could could command a room. And yet, after her disappearance she seemed to have the exact opposite effect. As if no mark had been made upon his memory by her presence.

THE LETTER

She rushed up the stairs. She threw her coat upon the bed, her hand upon the envelope. She drew the letter out unsteadily, unfolded the wrinkled page, and read:

Dear Amelia,

I enjoyed our recent lunch, and I hope it will be the first of many to follow. Please forgive me for not coming forward sooner. Had I suspected that you were as you said, "sufficiently recovered" I would have tried to reach you sooner. It was only my wish to respect your privacy which kept me from writing much earlier.

You may not be aware that for many years I was under the employment of Alexander Amela and Marion Clare Cinder, and during this time also made the acquaintance of their daughter, the photographer, Clara Amela, I pass this along in the hope that your acquaintance with her family might help resolve any question in the identity of your missing friend. As they have recently relocated nearby, I am enclosing their current address and phone. Certainly, the subject of their daughter's disappearance must be a difficult one, and I trust that you will approach them with all discretion.

———

The letter then went on to various non momentous details regarding current doings of "the chorus" and focusing on his upcoming opening, which he pressed her to attend in warm tones. She skimmed through all of this to see the letter was signed, "as always." Her first impulse was disbelief, and then, to find herself somewhat shocked. Why had he never mentioned before what he had all along known?

_____

Dear Mr. Amela and Mrs. Cinder,

Is your daughter alive? A few months ago she disappeared and I have been ill ever since. What was the nature of her disappearance? Please be assured that she has not been dead for ten years, as up until a few months ago I saw her nearly every day. She failed to mention that she had been for so long dead. I foolishly did not notice. Did you ever know her to be so untruthful? I don't mean to pry but it means very much to me to know whether or not she is the sort who would tell lies. She certainly did not seem so to me.

I have been living in a very small room, and have lost myself even within it's very walls. Marion, and Alexander, if I may call you by those names—I'm asking for your help, not as an admirer, an art critic, not for any selfish reason other than that your daughter is the dearest friend I have ever known.

———————

Dear Mr. Alexander and Mrs. Cinder,

Please forgive my previous letter. I've dearly regretted it ever since. You must think I have no heart to approach such a delicate matter so abruptly. Allow me to introduce myself. My name is Amelia.

Is your daughter alive?

———————

Dear Marion and Alex,

Have you ever wanted to know something so desperately that you'd go to any measure to find out. I am aware that I am stealing from you, by not representing myself to you correctly, by not being more careful in referring to your daughter's death (as I have just done again). I hope that you may find it possible to take pity upon me. If there were any other way, I assure you I would not bother you. Please inform me as soon as possible as to Clara's whereabouts, if you know them. If she is in fact dead, could you send me a photograph?

———————————

Dear Mrs. Cinder and Mr. Amela,

I am an acquaintance of your daughter, and an admirer of her photography. I am also an art critic and editor and am writing to you regarding a book I am editing and compiling on your daughter's photography tentatively titled "Acts of Levitation." It has been brought to my attention that you currently administer the rights to reproduce a large portion of her collection. I would be grateful for the opportunity to view some of these works for possible inclusion in the book. I would very much appreciate your assistance in this matter.

Sincerely,
Amelia Clare

She holds herself in glimmering repose. And thinks. I am well within this garden now.

Amelia has fallen asleep and found herself within a night garden where she rests beside these lilies her knees, these pansies her nose. Beside this violet her heart, once cloven.

Beginning here, where there are no other night palaces to inhabit. No other possessions to possess. No other interiors to ferret. No others to find her habitation. A song seems to drift from the rose garden which she hears and does not hear at all. Hiding within the hidden bloom. She is certain, if she can find the stepping stones which lead to the path behind the reflecting pool, beyond the orchards and to the rose garden, she is certain she will locate the source of sound.

But if it were only sound why did it wish to be tended? This garden where she rests beside an apparition.

A song flung towards any mirror. Other palaces have been plummeted. There remains only this construct. This mirror.

She states: The wind in every way prevents me from movement. My map is this day turned to darkness. My mind is hidden within these distant footsteps.

Here she dreams in tandem. The squirrels have abandoned the stream. Winter looms up in front of her. The hillside quivers. Her foot finds the wobbling stone, crosses the octagonal hazel grove, enters the sanctuary. She sits upon one end of a tattered seesaw, crouched against the earth. She sees a figure in the distance, approaching. Rises up. Once again her feet reach the ground. Her feet upon landing. She recalls the delicate arc of the air. The hesitation of heights. Her first excursion is barely remembered. The second, unexplained. The third, awaiting her. She steps through these three scenes of bodily absence.

The first room is muted, a childhood partition. She watches herself kneeling. Kneeling for what reason? She is kneeling beside her bed. What exactly has she seen? Delicate neck pressed against her chest. Hands pressed together in concentration. She can see the mind of the child, as if it were not her own. Her own mind pivots around from a center locked upon a distant reverie. She is attempting to transmit a message. To a girl in a house. Several streets away, she can imagine. The house echoes. She can see her footsteps. Tentative brown shingles. Three steps up to the screen door. She can see the geraniums in the flower box. The cracks in the cement upon which she stands. What is the message? She has lost all sense of herself. Her bare knees chafe against the carpet. Her toes numb, forgotten. Has the message been received? Footsteps intrude into the sanctuary. A voice and a figure demand her attention. Has the message been received? She thinks it has not. She feels her cold fingers now. Pins and needles in her heels. She senses the figure kneeling beside her. Drawing her hair away from her eyes. Soft white hands on her face. The look of concern. The child sees herself still, standing beside the flower box, tapping upon the window. The house, however, is empty. There is no sound from inside.

The second absence is a theater. Red light spills through a screen. Every row is filled. She hears loud laughter, a sort of banjo. A field of corn rises up before her. A dusty dog. She sees with perfect clarity "nothing" upon the screen. Then a set of sprinklers spinning. She is suddenly cold. She contemplates "red". Her shadow must follow her thought. The emptiness, she knows is not vacant, this nothing, a center. It appears to her first, as sky. Next, a wash of tumbling water. Her third approximation is a red field, and the theater disappears. The sounds drop away. She is walking into the field, and the red is made up of the nodding of tall undulating grasses. There is now an image in the midst of color. The image grows tired. Reclines. The stalks of grasses appear soft and dense from a distance, but up close each head has the consistency of a stiff paintbrush. She has escaped the redness by reclining within it. Her body makes a pattern. A carmine impression. Looking up for a moment she sees scaffoldings, ropes, curtains and lights. She closes her eyes and crosses her arms across her chest. Her own expression startles her. She is participating within the color. She has not planned this. But she knows now what she has not known before, that the color was meant to be entered. As the field begins to disperse she is aware that she has trespassed. It was not her red to be entered. She steps out of the field. Disentangles from the paintbrushes. She exits the theater with no pardon. Her impression in the field remains. Something of her conjecture is left. The tinge of the figure is noted. A method of blotting the audience. Obliterating the distance between theory and embodiment.

The third setting is out of doors. Pertaining to twilight. She stands outside of a brick building, with sloping lawns and wrought iron gates which seem to jut out at the observer. She gazes at the stalks of a magnificent terrace of roses, so old and elaborate that it's stalks are bold trunks with ample thorns. It is winter and no leaf or bloom adorn the complexity. The weight of this labyrinth lulls the entire maze to lie flat upon the sloping grounds. She thinks she can lift a bramble or two, and prop them. But the heaviness of their interwoven state prove the task hopeless.

She is standing merely gazing. A woman appears passing through the wrought iron gates. Without noticing Amelia she steps across directly to the lattice of rose branches, lifts one small branch, and surprisingly the tangle of stalks lifts along the entire length of the building. She balances the hedge until the roses have found their upright axis, properly set.

She awakens to music. Across her dim room. This startles her until she is coherent enough to recognize it is the sounds of her music box. And then she is once again alarmed. Has someone entered while she slept, and opened the box? The sheets are calmly cool, crumpled, surrounding her like water. Up to her shoulders. Her chin. She barely breathes.   But the room seems to breathe. She is alone.

Another vision in the garden, she silently wonders, recalling the shards of her dreams. The morning seems to be pierced with glass splinters. Numerous perforations. But the garden has vanished, and the darkness. Light bleeds through the thin shades outlining the windows. A branch tapping. The song is familiar. Sand being dropped slowly. A lullaby. She recalls the inscription. *A song which sleeps inside this box until needed.*

BEADS OF SILVER

Dear Ms. Clare,

Thank you for your letter and your interest in Ms. Amela's photographic art. As she is out of the country touring for several months I am currently managing her work. I would be happy to meet with you to discuss details about a possible book arrangement. Please contact my secretary (number below) at your convenience to set an appointment.

Sincerely,
Marion Cinder

Was she to assume that this meant that Clara was alive, and well? Who to believe was the recurring question which she patterned into the streets as she walked with growing anxiety towards the meeting. The meeting for which she herself must not be late. The other edge of the city, these multiple avenues, particularly unfamiliar. Not the streets but that she herself was unfamiliar among them. Particularly dressed in an attitude or expression far from habitual, and only as an attempt not to fall off into the gutters. She hurried somewhat, between pinched toes and cold noses, or so it appeared, glasses and stripes and flutter, between the carefully applied hats and lingerie. She hurried between falling matter, hail or premonitions. She hurried towards the white table linens and potted plants, toward the manicured fingers which greeted her. The crossed legs and shining expression of "call me Marion." Mrs. Cinder. She hurried towards and finally found herself seated across from a face, which if it had drawn itself completely open, might have echoed with familiarity. The ornamented hand reached her own, as if the hand clasping hers sought something greater. Greater than what, she wondered, finding her seat, placing her gaze gracefully across the room. Finding out where she had taken herself to exactly. She gazed then down towards the beaded water on the water glass filled with ice. The butter beads on the dainty silver dish beside the basket of bread.

She could progress no further than the basket of bread. Though she must look up and greet the vision.

The vision of a face, seemingly inquiring, then responding to what must be her own hesitation, softening. "Yes, call me Marion." Between the potted plants and the extraordinary weather, the waist fitted short coats of the waiters and trays carried perfectly at shoulder level. This was some other aspect of the city. "Call me Marion, Mrs. Cinder" was still beaming and waiting for her to begin, after all hadn't it been she who had arranged the meeting?

Finding her best impression of one very well at ease she grew taller and began speaking. The conversation she saw as an elegant obstacle course, something like walking through a crystal gallery accompanied by an ill mannered twin. Her object was to learn what she could, and reveal nothing. Since, after all that had occurred since her arrival, how could she know to whom she was actually speaking? What if "call me Marion" were merely a vision of a face, and the face behind that facade had long ago vacated? Who is to say that the photographs in her possession might not be deemed belonging to someone else? Could she have been Clara's mother? She could have been. Her object lost amidst the scenery. How to delicately point the question? Between potted plants and beads of silver.

"How did you come across her work?" Marion asked, as soon as there was a gap in their speech.

"In the Capital Letters Gallery, years ago."

"I see. Now tell me about the project of the book. It is a book you are interested in? She's told me nothing about it. I'm very curious." She said with lifted brow. "How did you meet?"

Amelia paused, carving herself a corner from which to reflect, "we have friends in common." So as to avoid any further questions, she went on to describe in great detail the small communities which surrounded several notable galleries.

Marion nodded through this account. She had only wanted to gather a better notion of who she was dealing with.

"As for the book," Amelia continued on, relieved at having gotten past that maneuver, "there are a number of portraits I'm interested in. It will be hard cover, limited edition of course, and coordinated with a large opening if all goes as planned."

Marion seemed pleased. "Very ambitious. Will there be text as well?"

"Yes, I'm in the process of writing."

"A writer, you didn't tell me. Excellent" she said, with the sense that she could now press her into a pattern, and perhaps explain her appearance which was not exactly what she had expected.

The conversation continued, between baskets of bread, sharp hesitation, and faltering silences. Marion carried an abundance of quick smiles and manners. Amelia was studying her adeptness, wondering when she could insert her question, and how to it casually. Finally there was an opening which seemed appropriate. Marion had gotten onto the subject of her daughter's recent departure, and how often it falls upon her to handle all of the details of her career.

"Do you have an address so I might contact Ms. Amela directly?" she asked.

Marion was quick to reply. "Oh that won't be necessary. I'm quite happy to handle details. If you'll tell me exactly which pieces you are interested in, I'll let you know where they are located and how to arrange things."

Amelia now began to panic. She wondered what other imaginary project she would need to invent in order to find an address for Clara. But then she realized that something close to the truth would do just as well. She hesitated again. Then began, "You are very generous to meet me. I'm very much looking forward to working with you."

"And I as well" Marion returned, lifting her glass.

I'd also like to send a personal letter, if you don't mind. It's just been ages since we've been in touch."

"Oh certainly. I'd be happy to—" And she stopped there dabbing her lips with her napkin.

"Where is she now?" she tossed off casually.

Marion looked up. "Oh, if only I could remember such things." She laughed as if to apologize. "I do have her itinerary at home. So many places I'm afraid I can't keep track day to day. If one's mother does not know then I guess you could say nobody can keep up with her." And then she drifted again, laughing delicately, somewhere between the desire to reveal herself and the desire to question.

The conversation went on to Amelia's interests in art and writing, but mostly tended towards Marion's new business which Amelia had a difficult time understanding exactly. She knew it had something to do with travel as they began with their salads, had determined that transporting fine art was part of the project when their soufflés arrived and over coffee and tarts began to think that she arranged tours through various international galleries. She expressed each particular with an impressive air, a wonderful cadence, and the type of authority that Amelia wouldn't think to question. She glimpsed Clara here and there between the calculated asides, between courses and directives. Something about the eyes. Somewhere she had been found. She, seeming merely another semblance. It would take another several meetings perhaps. If she could manage.

LETTER TO CLARA

I have emerged from the corners of the room.

You cannot disappear entirely. You've left a teacup in the studio.

You've left the lying mirror.

I saw the shadow across your face, but as soon as I approached it vanished.

There is this sparkling silence all around you now.

You've devastated my borders. I am being carried.

The light lilts. The picture moves away.

This isn't your name, but since you won't tell me—.

You've disappeared inside the rose.

My lip is not a comma.

My hands will finally obey.

But how did she get on when the other did not return? The question after all begs a larger location as it grows to fill arcing days. Nobody knew. Nobody could send any word to unlock the location of the question, which she carried until she plummeted fatigued, as if within an iron cloak. The chorus related only that they had seen her move into the street, below the city gates. With a battered suitcase. Then they all said that she had died, fallen into the dark winter days.

Fallen into the days? But how did she return the question after all? Nobody knew. The arcing days plummeted. They all said the winter days could do that, abstract the notion of swimming. But must the dark portrait be everywhere, she asked?

I don't think so, answered the swallow.

So she took the dearest thing she owned, the black portfolio and walked quite alone, to the gates of the river. She kissed the leopard, who was asleep upon the banks. She reached the river and it seemed to her the billows nodded so oddly, as if answering her question. Have these portraits been dissolved upon your asking? If I drown the image will I be returned the reflections which lie within? She must have supposed she had received an answer, since she threw the portfolio into the dark oily waters, but it fell very near, with all of the glossy images spilling upon the banks, half submerged. It was as if the river did not want to cover the pictures entirely.

But now she thought she had not thrown them far enough and she must correct her mistake. She had not nodded entirely to the winter day. She knelt upon the banks and bowed her head to reach the images dissolving softly, and as she leaned across she heard a voice.

Why give yourself to water? she asked.

You misunderstand me, the girl answered with her gaze. By this time the woman had coaxed her upon dry land and into her house with very black doors, lofty ceilings, and pristine straight backed chairs. She turned the latch in the polished fitting as she closed the door behind them. It was as if the river had never existed. Daylight shone strangely within the intricately paneled walls of gray and white. The walls were covered with such lovely portraits and the girl was encouraged by her hostess to gaze at each as long as she liked. She gazed deeply, disappearing into the images until she had almost forgotten why she had thrown the others into the river.

She was made very comfortable by the woman who moved from room to room as elegantly as if she had been made to walk between two long panes of glass. She was correct in her glances and intonations, she was gracious in each chamber, at each hour of the day. She seemed genuine in her affection for the girl who moved as if within a daze from room to room, through the days and nights admiring one image after another hung perfectly upon the walls. How spacious and grand were the rooms. Every conceivable mood seemed to meet her own within the images which drew her in tentatively until each had drowned. She had seen almost every corridor, every room and hall. The doors stood ajar. The days fell open. Her malady forgotten.

o

She studies a pastoral scene in oils. A woman in billowing rose skirt and peasant blouse reaching her arms up along the trunk of a leaning tree. Two small children at her feet. The atmosphere is golden and the trees washed in twilight.

o

A young boy walks barefoot through a winter's night. Angels pat his ankles to keep them warm.

o

A young woman reclines beside a window, clasping a small volume to her chest and looking through the glass.

o

In black and white pencil, the winds are bound with a sewing thread.

o

A scholar mistakes a flower for a bird.

o

A miniature etching of an endless field of wheat.

o

After what had seemed an afternoon, but had actually been a series of elaborate weeks and turnings, there began to emerge the sense that although she had seen so many magnificent portraits that one in particular was missing. She noticed and asked, "Why is this door not falling open, as all of the others upon my approach?"

The woman answered oddly by turning the subject elsewhere, to the hands of the clock. But each day the girl circled the locked door and then tentatively turned the handle, which fit perfectly, as all the others, within the palm of her hand. Again and again she asked her hostess, whose perfect good humor seemed to dwindle, and when the question fell upon her countenance her face grew somewhat drawn, until finally she saw that it was no use, that her guest would not stay without the answer to this one question which plagued her.

The woman pointed out as if in warning, "It is not exactly polite to one's hostess to leave her absolutely no privacy whatsoever."

The girl was taken aback. It was true, that she was merely a guest within this house. It did not belong to her, nor did it's contents, and she did not have any right to claim the generosity and attentions of her hostess. When she fell from her trance—from portrait to portrait—to this realization of what she had been demanding, her trailing steps drew her to a window for the first time in many months, and there she stood with eyes darting out into the actual landscape she had almost lost sight of entirely.

She remembered then the portfolio she had thrown into the water, and what she had wished for in return. She decided it was time to return to the river, to retrieve her question where she had once placed it. It had been a relief to momentarily release it. Her limbs felt wonderfully strong again, as they had not felt in months. Her mind was clear and weightless, until she began to draw near the question, which converted her trailing steps to those more firmly planted with concern.

o

She followed one portrait after another, searching for clues. Shall I retrace my steps, she asked first of a small photograph, in sepia tones. A white-haired woman embraces the side of a dollhouse. Near it's entrance on the table are miniature motorbikes and a stiff doll. Her expression is one of grief. But how can one grieve for a house, and not even a real house, she wondered.

o

Overhanging a narrow cobbled wall is an old and ruinous chateau. Thick vines grow up around the walls of pink granite. A moat cuts through the grounds and at one edge a small party sets out in little boats.

o

A man stands in front of an iron gate, shoes and cane pointing towards the camera.

o

Two women sit in a cloth chair outside upon a balcony. The sun is in their faces. I know you, says one convulsively to the other. I'm not certain the other returns, looking away.

o

A child sits upon the back of a reindeer, leaping. The child's hair spills out behind her. She wears a long blue coat, the same color as the eye of the deer, who turns it's head to look back at her.

o

She had nothing to collect for her departure, since she had arrived with nothing, and so she collected her recollections and arranged them carefully. The girl pinning a sailboat to a cliff was placed delicately beside a three color sea. The blind bird who slept in the hollow was tucked discretely beside the bright Parisian street scene. She kept also the glossy green color of ribbon which tied the hair of a sleeping child. She filled her memory with bits of this sort, the numbers of brush-strokes, how many steps she had taken down each corridor. The number of wingbeats it had taken a storm to reach a shore.

When all was in order for her departure as well as she could manage, she went to her hostess who she found for the first time reclining in the center of the day. As she bent to clasp her hands and give thanks she noticed that the woman had pressed an iron key into her hands. She knew at once what this meant, and instantly regretted her earlier behavior. The eyes of the woman met her own and she was suddenly certain that all along she had intended to eventually let her view the locked room. If only she had contained her impatience, then she might have known gracefully. Nevertheless, she followed her own fleeting footsteps beside those of the woman advancing towards the staircase and up towards the locked room, passing portrait after magnificent portrait as they went. They reached the door finally and out of habit before trying the key, she reached her hand around the doorknob. She felt it perfectly fitting to the palm of her hand as before, but this time it fell open easily.

At first she saw nothing as the light which was coming through windows on three sides of the room was so bright that she was momentarily blinded. The light spilled out into the hallway and filled the whole house. They stepped into the room which was immaculate. The paneling neatly painted in three shades of gray, all the furniture in order, the fireplace imposing. The windows came into focus now, as if they'd stopped moving. The dimensions of the room fell into place and all was suddenly still. There was however not a single portrait on any of the walls.

A PHOTOGRAPH IN BLACK AND WHITE

The day arrived for the next meeting which was to take place at Mrs. Cinder's home in the same distant neighborhood of potted plants. Amelia was punctual, moving briskly from train to street, training her eyes upon the present and even more nervous than before. After all, if this were her family, there would exist some evidence. She would have been found out utterly. There could be no more question about identity. There could be none of the stuttering to find one's place. Her place would be found, or certainly would not. She imagined all of this in detail as she ascended up the stone steps to the iron gates and pressed the buzzer firmly. She was greeted by Marion. Was this Marion? Marion who had been tucked and pressed and precise was now somewhat beige and asymmetrical. Amelia, by comparison felt stiff in her carefully chosen ensemble. But the house seemed to welcome her.

They sat and talked mildly for several minutes before the discussion of the book, and Amelia was enjoying this. She admired the attitude of the house, which was drawn and very postured and bright. Engulfed by curtains and flower arrangements. This other city not inhabited with loud radiators and scurrying mice, but instead wide clear windows and teal painted walls, contrasting the mahogany window frames. She was shown several rooms. First cherrywood imposing. Then charcoal. A lemon divan upon slate marble.

She shook inwardly recognizing several of Clara's photographs on the walls: the textured urchin series, set against bronze, the morning dove interiors in the gray room. There were several others she did not recognize which she assumed to be hers as well: Cross Sections of Telephone Landscapes, and then the Curious Sea Coasts, light dropping between outcroppings of silver rock. Marion was leading her through the house, scarves trailing, looking over her shoulder, eyes liquid, pale. Then at the sound of a tiny bell, left her for several moments in a large bright room filled with what appeared to be Clara's work.

Silver prints in various washes. Silver turned jet black. Five of them were covered with silver thread and the sixth with a bonnet. Then a handful of flaming straw.

But as she stepped closer she saw what she had not expected. The signature was an unfamiliar etching, of which she could only make out the letter K. And then another. And another. A vermilion storm. A hand of silver and foot of bronze. A city disappearing into waves.

But she recognized these—they must be Clara's. Still the signature, unrecognizable.

In one of the upstairs bedrooms she finally saw what she had hoped most to see. To know to whose house she had come. A photograph of Clara beside a young woman sitting on a stone bench. There could be no doubt. She realized, entranced in front of the image, that there could be no more indefinite questioning. She had in fact found the person she was looking for. She was not merely vapor, a monogram, a faulty mirror. None of this had been imagined. She had come near to doubting she had ever embraced such a creature. She knew a moment of solitary calm, and it was then she realized that it hadn't been so much to find her, as to find that she had a history. This made her actual.

Mrs. Cinder saw her admiring the photograph. "Lovely shot? That was almost, let me see—thirteen years ago now" she said oddly fingering the curtain, "which seems impossible." And then she looked vacant and odd.

She looks as if she did last week, or yesterday as I might imagine her, Amelia thought. But she said nothing of course. Of course, she thought, as if she could have stood there another thirteen years, to see if the photograph would age.

They stood there quietly for a minute, until Marion returned from her reverie and directed them back to the living room. "You've brought something with you." she said, nodding towards the portfolio.

"Yes."

"Shall we look?" she asked moving across the room in her willowy manner. A walk which she recognized too well. The inclination of her head which she had memorized.

Amelia lifted up the portfolio onto a large table and they both stood over it. She had meant to pull each one out gracefully and to arrange them, but her hand slipped and they all spilled out at once, at which point both women began arranging the images simultaneously. There was the first instant or two when nothing could be actually seen, and then Marion's face had gone completely expressionless. She said nothing but then looked up at Amelia demanding something which she could not guess. Marion turned away from the images and sat down. Amelia followed, concerned with what would come next.

Marion looked at her, glared at her actually. "What is this?" she asked, in a strained whisper.

Searching her eyes somewhat desperately. She knew her reserve was about to collapse. "I don't know what you are asking." she faltered, twisting her limbs as she said so.

She asked, "Where did you find those photographs?"

This scene, she thought, is it echoing another? She looked down as if her hands had become transparent. Did she shiver or did the whole room seemed to sigh? "I told you, that they were given to me." she said concentrating on the surface of the table, noticing that it was still flat. Seeing the walls remain static, she almost expected them to lurch and reel. But that would not happen again. She watched the room into correctness.

Marion was going on, "Yes I know, but who gave them to you? Certainly Katherine did not. I don't know why you have not been straightforward with me. But I insist that you tell me." She had taken back her more formal tone.

Katherine, she wondered, who was Katherine? Amelia was somewhat intimidated, but also truly lost. "I never said that Katherine had given them to me," she heard herself saying. She was thinking, I never did know her. She was never known.

"Who else?" Marion asked, "This book is on Katherine's work, is it not? And you are an acquaintance of hers—didn't you tell me that as well?"

"No," she said slowly in response, I never mentioned Katherine." She thought back to the photograph upstairs. "Who is Katherine?" she asked.

"My daughter," Marion answered genuinely confused.

Amelia began to piece together a shroud. Her daughter? Was Katherine Clara's sister then? The K. in the signature she did not recognize?

She once again found herself nowhere. And still they sat there silent. Amelia could barely contain herself.

"It was Clara" she said very quietly. "It was Clara who gave me the photographs."

Marion looked at her in disbelief. "Then why if it was Clara? Why would you ask for an address? Is it possible you couldn't know? You do know don't you? How long has it been since—"

Amelia looked at her tentatively, "It was Clara. The book is to be about Clara" she kept repeating. She had to keep repeating in order to keep the walls and the floors aligned. She could not believe all she had been brought through, but she was determined to keep the room intact.

"When did she give them to you?" There was a corner in Marion's eye. Small, unmistakable.

The small corner brought her back. She saw finally, it is not only I who have lapsed. She searched this corner and there she saw Katherine. Sitting silent like a bird, upon a stone bench. And there she saw Clara, leaping up from her place beside her sister. She saw the empty space in her eye which had once been occupied. In all of this time she was silent. But then she answered. "Several months ago I saw her last."

Marion's eye vanished and reappeared without clarity. Without liquid. "You must understand that this is very difficult for me," she said. "I don't know whether to believe you. I want to very much."

Katherine, who is Katherine, she repeated to herself. She realized that Katherine had swallowed up the house. The scent of her everywhere. The other daughter lost among other hopes abandoned. Was Katherine an artist of some magnitude? No she was not, Marion's gaze told her. Clara had been more hopeful, but then Clara was nowhere. And that is why, Amelia thought, Marion was so eager to meet me. Because Katherine was suddenly somewhere. Katherine is the other side of Clara, she thought.

From here all attempts at conversation failed until it became clear they were tossing back and forth vague impressions of a loss intolerable. Amelia saw this third version of Marion revealed, the one who had never recovered.

"If there were something I could tell you." Marion said, "We always knew there was a possibility she simply didn't want to be found."

Amelia watched her slip to disbelieving. "Is it possible she's never been found?" she asked. But she was given no answer.

It was all too much for Marion. An hour before she had been on the verge of finding something. But she wouldn't allow herself. She was now beige and impenetrable.

Marion removed herself a few more leagues, gathered her reserves and said to the photographs, "No I don't recognize these." She looked at Amelia and said, "I'm sorry, but I've no question it isn't my daughter you knew. The photographs must be impressions made after her own. Best to leave them with me" she paused, concentrating her now controlled gaze "you understand, to avoid any further confusion."

MARION

13 June 2001

Dearest Alex,

I am writing to you from my bedside in the morning after you have departed with Katherine. I am already most anxious to know how you have survived your trip and how you find the seaside cottage. Is everything as we planned? Are the red roses in bloom? Do the stone steps echo as they always did before? How was Katherine during the trip? Did either of you manage to rest? Is it wonderful to be in Brittany again? Did all of the artwork arrive undamaged? I now must stop plaguing you with questions.

The more that I consider our decision, the more strongly I feel that we've made the right choice for Katherine. Although I know we have both had our doubts, I think we were right to follow our inclinations. After all, why shouldn't she inherit her sister's legacy? There is nothing we could do for Clara—poor dear. It pains me to say her name. But upon discovering all of those hidden pieces—Katherine did discover them, and that is hardly a step away from having created them herself. If she believes she did so herself, what harm can there be in going along with it? It took little to convince her, after all. There is so much of her memory which is still a fright. A summer abroad is what she most needs and who knows, maybe being surrounded by art will inspire her to take up drawing again.

Please forgive me, love, for bringing up this subject which we agreed not to discuss again. This all comes up only because I've been bothered by another inquiry into Clara's work, but this time I was approached by someone with originals in hand. I've no idea how she got them, and only responded to her letter assuming she was interested in Katherine. I could not convince her to leave them with me, though I tried everything short of tears. In any case, the second meeting was awkward enough. She will not bother us again. I'm convinced she'll do nothing with the pieces, as she is under the delusion that Clara gave them to her not long ago. My dear we must devise some plan to keep away these ill individuals.

Here I will soon be busy with details for the upcoming show. Sadly I will miss both of you. But I will let you rest now. Kiss Katherine for me and take her out to sit on the rocks at low tide.

Love to you
Marion

II.

KATHERINE

The light blinks, not less obviously. This house, and it's projections, inhabitants, habit. The night and it's linking to loss. There are sheets of coldness, a paralyzed type of grappling with the monuments as they slide.

Out on the pier, dropping between scattered islands and darker land which is obliged to scatter the light. I sat between myself and the shore, and there less obviously the waves upon that quest unbeknownst to the object.

Unknown to me falling forms of ashes fill the room. The room is full with presence. A chair sleeps quietly in a corner. All of these masks are open vials of chatter. So busy in speech one may be drowned. I may be in a foreign country but certain boundaries don't recall themselves. I am inside this house, but the house has internalized me. I cannot exactly speak about what is happening. The table stands where it is. The nights mold presence until I can no longer remember nights. They become heavy objects, and I carry them as I carry about my sister's head.

o

We sat around the table drinking scotch and Pear William, but the table never did sit. I wished to go out for a walk. But certainly the house would draw me back. Where was one supposed to sleep otherwise? I considered the cathedral with it's stone spires delicately carved in a semblance of Breton lace. I considered the streets. I considered a hotel. I even considered that we depart for home this very night.

My mind is not violet, as the rose geraniums in the courtyard. Their soft green leaves in stenciled flounces mark their scent upon my fingers. The true roses which line the house are the same as those one finds all over France. The color is unmistakable. At crossroads, marking some event past. Blood, unduplicatable. It does not cross borders.

The desk sleeps within a corner. Only the bathroom and kitchen are uninhabited. But how to exist there? Still too many comings and goings. I prodded the old stone of the basement. Unwired the locked doors to the servant's quarters and found them full of extra beds. I uncaught the latch to the pigeonaire, and found children's drawings on a small desk in a corner. Were they of her hand? I saw from there an open passage in the ceiling, leading to the stone attic. I walked down the heavy stone stairs. Marked the places where the floorboards were lose and creaking. I took one perfectly round stone, and hid it in a particular vase so it would no longer keep me up at night. I was certain that nobody else in the house had seen. And so if I hear again, at night, the stone dropping and rolling across the floors, I will know.

I hung drying herbs I had gathered up on each of the four sides of my large bedroom. Mostly hypericum perforatum, which translates "over an apparition." I aired the linens and opened the windows. I left the door open, the lights on. I gave up the idea of sleep, and read instead until I grew tired, but I never did grow tired. I would lie in the bed and close my eyes tight, every muscle tensed. This was my refusal to see anything that might appear before me. I might hear, but would not purposefully look. I felt more permeable than I desired to be. I wrung the water from my hair but the worry from my hands could not be so easily persuaded.

The swallows are present and fly in the patterns of my thoughts. The seagulls and crows wake me. Horse hoofs on cobblestones accompanied by jingling. This could be any time, I thought. I could be another. In the midst of a squall I dreamed something comforting, which escapes me. That the house was no longer somewhat in ruins. I saw it in it's splendor. And everywhere red rich fabrics though the stone hearth still bare.

I heard the church bells. A shutter slammed in the wind. Father asked if I had heard anything last night. No, I answered, although I had not slept. The wind was ever-present. I misunderstood Alain, the French artist who lives in a neighboring cottage, when he said, the problem here is "the wines." What, I asked perplexed. "The winds" he had said, the problem here is the winds. Did they keep him awake as well?

I am no longer enamored with old stone, with narrow streets and gothic arches. The weight of the old like so much suffocation. There is death in that type of beauty, the coldness and immovability of what has past. The lives that have lived here are etched into the walls. The stone exhales and exhausts me with it's memory. The lives of the dead outnumber the lives of the living. So how must the living claim the space in which to be numerous?

The present contains the past as well as the future, occurs continually in the same place and time. In this sense I am the inhabitants of the house, and the house is myself. If I do not admire the behavior of the presences I must reprimand myself as well. Some will not behave in a manner befitting the dead. The living will not acknowledge that they are outnumbered. And so I sit here with numerous uninvited guests, all eager to inhabit my story.

I tell what I know. What I know is very small, and what I can tell of that more diminutive.

A stone house breeds dampness. It rained for an hour or so last night and the first floor was flooded. The place seems unreal. Liquid hallways. This room is never bright. Not even in the middle of the day on the brightest days.

The nets and stranded boats. The sails. The coast looks clear with standing stones. A seagull perched atop a stranded boat.

I was walking out in the garden and I heard steps behind me, beside the rose geraniums, the sound of steps through water. Without turning I saw her white skirts billowing. Her hair trailing water behind her. Her bare legs twisted with seaweed. A blue finger upon my shoulder.

o

The fireplace is stalking me. Now within the light I am able to speak of the placid pools of seawater below. There was rain again. I looked back into the room twice. The firescreen shivered. I was frozen somewhat and could not get undressed or braid my hair. Father appeared, hearing me move about, and said somewhat mockingly, listen to this music my dear and stop your teeth from chattering. How could he possibly protect me from that which he did not even recognize?

I flew out of the room in a rage, covers streaming behind me. This empty room is empty except for myself, supposing that. The trembling shutter. I refuse to sleep in the room which was hers. As a child, she would leave her room, as I had just done, and climb into the small bed with me, and then while we lay awake she would tell me about the ghosts of three women she had seen, who told her that they had all been in love with a priest in this house which was originally a rectory. One with red hair, the other with a bonnet, and a third holding a child. It was the priest who scraped chairs along the floors at night, Clara would insist. But even on those occasions when we ran upstairs and took all of the chairs out of the rooms above us the sounds still had continued to keep us awake.

Mostly she'd seen the women near the hearth—tending the fire—that rattling firescreen which is now covered. The chimney is sealed shut. So I know it could not be the wind, despite Alain's suggestion. There is a sealed room which lies behind the hearth which can only be entered by climbing out the window and along a little ledge below the eaves. We imagined they were once locked away there.

One time she said she saw all three of them leaning over me while I slept. When I recall this, there can be no reasoning with me. I have tried to convince myself to banish the fears of my childhood, and father has encouraged me—though with little success since he has no understanding of my experience. He told me on more than one occasion it would be foolish to waste the loveliest of rooms. This is his idea of comforting me. Of course it is of no use. He had never spent a night in that room, being as he claimed too well ensconced on an upper floor. I retreated into the middle smaller room which once was mine. The smaller room had correspondingly a smaller bed. Father looked at me oddly and said, your choices are fair. I knew I had no choice at all, and that I might perhaps regret it if I determined to give up the large lovely room as I stood in stocking feet, the small room all the while closing in around me. The paneling makes it seem smaller still. I got into the narrow bed determined to sleep with the lights on trying to forget the nonsense of being stalked by a firescreen. I promised myself as much. But then the door swung open. I must have dozed off. She should have swam ashore. I can still see her now as I write, hair dripping down her back. A puddle on the old wooden floors.

I felt cold air in the room circulating. In the evenings we laughed around the bright yellow dining room, but then in my own secret dread I would wait for the sounds to begin. Last night they were subdued, it was only the firescreen, and I deliberately did not speak of it all through dinner. The rain was coming down once again. I was frightened last night at the way my heart leapt about the room. Then lying alone in the narrow bed, father opened the door and I shuddered. He had knocked, he said, I must not have heard. And it was only to say good-night. I slept for some time and remembered white skirts billowing on the dredging posts when I woke.

JOURNAL— 13 JUILLET

The landscape is green moss and brown. Green algae and brown mud, and gray silver pools with stretches of rock which stand and rise in clusters. It is all rain today in the tidal sanctuaries. Those out walking are certain to have regrets.

Which version of rain do you know? To tell the obvious. To tell the telling nights. I can see from here what I could not see before. If I could sleep in this room I would choose to do so. I went out with a shovel and came back with the tide.

Alain showed me a heart urchin, dug into a pail. It's breathing hole sunk. There are more interruptions here, but no matter. The tide is a symptom. The rain rolls off and is blown over a stone wall. The sunken sea. He showed me a living heart urchin all covered in fur.

I talk to myself beside the pool of seawater, because I am tired. And yet I worry over the tidal pools. The colors, now that the rain has cleared, are magnificent. Azure with patches of clarity which look inviting, though the water is numbing even in summer.

JOURNAL—15 JUILLET

My small handwritten journal with the transparent gold flower on the cover seems brighter; though it is small and incremental it is very present, and not weighted down with the project of accomplishing anything. I see someone walking again out on the stone wall. Looking for what? But I might be mistaken in what I am seeing. The window shudders as I approach.

Look, the tide has come in. The ships are afloat. There are many sailboats out in the morning. And now that I am here looking out over the water, I feel as if I could stay. I hear footsteps again, out along the seawall.

Another night in the small protected middle room heard nothing if little at all. The presences for some reason avoid this room, thank goodness. The sea is misted over. When to enter the other room to fetch possessions I am swarmed, being watched. The floorboards speak. I am being watched certainly, and they are imitating my movements somewhat mockingly and somewhat out of genuine curiosity. They partially think I am trying to claim their space with a series of archaic rituals. I light my candle and place herbs in all four corners. I always know when it is that I have overstayed my limit and they wish me to be gone. I took a little bit longer today and whenever my attention lapsed I could feel their eyes pressing. Also on the floor above I heard footsteps. And no one was upstairs I am certain because father was asleep in the room next to mine. The firescreen spoke only once. Then in the afternoon when I was downstairs in the kitchen I heard doors slamming. By this time father had gone out. It was windy, as usual, so I went about the house and latched all of the windows and doors. Then I sat quietly with my infusion of tilleul, until the doors began to slam again, at which point I fetched my sunhat and went outside, refusing to remain within this presence any longer. None of this do I tell anyone, convinced as I am that my confessions only encourage my discomfort.

There is now the breathing ghost and I will not tell anyone about this since I now know that is what she prefers. I was in the small safe room reading alone and heard soft breathing as if it were very close to my ear. When I lifted my eyes and turned my head in the direction of the sounds they stopped abruptly. I listened to the silence and heard nothing. But as soon as I turned my head and focused my eyes once again on the page, which I did mechanically, without thought, as if it had been done for me, the breathing began again. It was not threatening—though extremely disconcerting. Then it seemed to follow me into the big room later that day. I was standing near the window and once again I heard and felt the breath along my ear. I listened closely to be certain that it was not my own breath that I heard. I held my breath for a moment, and still I heard this other breath very nearby.

White skirts billowing. I jump off of the boat and my arm is about her neck. I am swimming and everything is blue. Water. Sky. Her face is blue. And then the water begins to feel warm. There are voices. Whose voices do I hear? She used to say she could walk just above the water. She could walk out to the small island even when the tides were in. I carry my sister's head. The dream is always the same.

There is almost nothing to tell today of the quietness of the inhabitants, but they did lock us out of the house, and also the doors continue to slam. It is true the wind carries many things, shutters, doors, and curtains, but I have felt the deliberate presence which assists a door in it's flight, and it was not wind.

There was something else I wanted to add but I can not remember and as I sit in my room, the small safe room, and this particular thought vanishes, I think to myself that I will remember to write it down later because it is such an important memory. But now I can remember nothing and I think that they are stealing my thoughts, as well as my sleep. I feel assured that they are quiet because I no longer inhabit the large room. I am allowed to store some clothing there, but nothing else is permissible.

JOURNAL—23 JUILLET

Last night, on the stair, I was standing in my doorway, looking at the landing, and I heard footsteps on the stone stairs right in front of me, but saw nothing. I stood there too stunned to move, thinking that maybe someone would appear- person or ghost, but when none did I finally moved within and closed the door to my room.

In the morning I slept fitfully, and in the afternoon I went out for a walk to the chapel, and on my return, saw

Alain out in his immaculate garden. He invited me for a glass of kir, which I gratefully accepted and we sat, beside the rhododendrons talking of many things. He is a very considerate listener, and before I knew what I was doing I found myself close to divulging all that had been occurring of late. I realize that this is questionable behavior on my part, but when I look back I realize that my secrecy has begun to be as difficult as my discomfort.

Instead of revealing all, I managed though to turn the conversation towards the subject of historical ghosts. He was not at all a skeptic, and neither did he dismiss the subject, or lunge towards it with that fanatical zeal of those who one knows one has made a mistake to mention it, since they will speak of nothing else on any other occasion as long as others are not present. Instead he told me of the woman dressed in mourning, often seen out walking along the little path that leads to the seawall. It is said that she lost her husband at sea close to three hundred years ago. I asked him then, what if anything he had felt in his cottage, which we know to have been built in the same period as ours, about 1604. He told me that he came to the house having heard stories about it's former inhabitants, with much skepticism, but also with curiosity, which he fears has tinged his objectivity. I asked him if he believes now, that his house is inhabited. He said he does not believe that a ghost would speak in the manner that these inhabitants speak. Then I asked what it was he had experienced. His answer stays beside me at unexpected moments when I find myself wondering what these presences require of me. The impressions of memories of others left behind, he called them, seen through the lens of the personal psyche.

I realized today, that when we arrived and I original-ly took the inhabited room, there was a painting on the mantelpiece which I did not particularly like. It was a landscape of pale greens outlined in deep blue. But then father discovered that the other side of the canvas was painted as well. It was a portrait of a woman's face, which I can recall now, not very clearly since I dare not study her carefully, except that she had brown hair, and a ker-chief tied over her head. We both liked this side of the canvas and so left it on the mantle. Now it occurs to me that turning this canvas over as we did may have served as a signal. I'm tempted to turn the painting over.

JOURNAL—26 JUILLET

Concentration broken or lapsed. A door is opened and closed. If I sit here, what is it I might accomplish? At the hour for tea I may recount. All of those books of con-sequences. The page is set and somewhat torn. As is this horizon.

I've visited the nearby library, with broken chairs. I look out the window on one side and a shadow passes over the waters. I look out the other side and a little courtyard is all covered with rain. There are signs in the library reminding visitors to use the phantoms, beside the secret door which leads down another stone staircase and passes a glass window with diamonds of green and blue. Phantoms, I wondered? The library was old, and I soon began to watch my shadow, to notice the accumulation of dust along the glass cases, and to notice the way the floor would creak in several places at once when anyone crossed the floor. I also watched the bronze bust of the library's major benefactor, square in the middle of room, who seemed to watch the movements of all within. But soon I learned that a "phantom" is only the French name for a wooden board which marks the place from where you have borrowed a book. There is also a bronze bust of the founder of the establishment, born in 1610, who is said to open and close certain glass cabinets on occasion.

The mist lifts a bit. I see pale green yellow in the water. As the tide begins to lilt out. Never is it motionless, as these notions I cling to. Footsteps in time with my thinking.

JOURNAL—27 JUILLET

All is quiet virtually. Cold air rushes from a room but then the windows are empty. Sounds are heard on the stair, but most certainly someone is home. A dim light protrudes from the old servants' quarters, the door of which is wired shut. But it must be a light coming from behind windows within. The hearth in the inhabited room is noisy, but then it must have been the wind.

Last night we had a wonderful dinner of galettes. Then we sat drinking creme de cassis in the parlor and I continued making collages out of playing cards.

This day, this estuary apart. We walked to the store and carried home rhubarb compote, crepes, eggplant and tomatoes, along with bread and cheese. We walked down the long dirt roads through artichoke fields past old stone homes guarded by the minutest of little dogs.

This is an account of how I gave up my lovely room, and much of my sleep (I who am enamored of sleep) during a summer of noisy ghosts.

I hope I will be able to remember all since there is much to record. I approached the mantle with trepidation, since this is where most of the noises center. I looked at the woman's portrait. She seemed somewhat menacing now that I had realized her intent. She did not look back at me. I touched the portrait hesitantly. Then I turned it over. I was concerned at touching it. Did not relish the notion. But when I had turned it over the seascape suddenly appeared abstract. I could not tell which way it was oriented. And all the while panicking for touching the portrait itself. I had remembered it as horizontal, but it seemed to be vertical. Finally I was able to collect myself to see that the portrait was vertical. I had had it reversed though. I set the portrait as it should be and retreated from the room. I could only do this during the day time since a few days earlier the light had extinguished. Another sign that we were not welcome in the room, especially during the night. That was a couple of days ago. Then yesterday morning I went into the room and found that the portrait had been reversed so that the face of the woman again appeared. I stopped in my steps not wanting to believe what I saw in front of me. I began to wonder who this woman was and how her portrait had gotten into the room. But soon I pressed on with my morning rituals and became absorbed enough to forget the portrait momentarily. Later in the day I snuck back into the room and turned the portrait around again.

I see now, she doesn't want me touching the portrait. The portrait is also hers. All of them are hers. And the ones that are missing, the small portfolio which together we'd chosen and put together. I have given up searching for that.

Last night I was standing in a phone booth in the village, with the ocean to my left and the cathedral with it's stone spires to my right. I was speaking to my mother who was asking for further details of how I was getting on, if I had been sleeping. Her questions seemed endless. She said as I stood in the booth and cars rushed past on the cobblestones, 'I hear the French gull through the wires'. He needn't be so loud to dramatize his point.'

Her attempt at humor did not move me. I was already disturbed by a scene I had witnessed earlier that day, walking in the Jardin Exotique with Alain. A large Rhodesian ridgeback had nearly seriously injured a small girl. The dog snapped at her, whose mother pulled her back just in time to save her from worse. "He isn't a very nice dog", the little girl told it's owner once she had stopped crying. He was sadly too full of affection for the dog to see the danger which had been escaped. The child's face had been grazed and was bleeding. I tried for several hours to let this image fall from my mind, the grotesque dog's face, the child's face streaked with tears and blood, standing before a diamond of heady sunflowers. Alain, however was a great distraction. He guided me through the circular paths, through figure-eights of fuschia's, and groves of hazelnuts, past anchors and old canoes placed decoratively among roses, displaying his vast knowledge of horticulture until I had almost forgotten. But the scene came back to me, as I stood there in the booth at dusk.

To make matters worse mother insisted on discussing the ghosts in the chateau, something I distinctly try to avoid before bedtime, and especially since I knew that father would be asleep very early, as was his habit. Mother has been sworn to secrecy about what she calls "my visions" and I've not gone into much detail not wishing to upset her. Still I wish that I had never spoken of it. As we talked I looked towards the cathedral, and noticed huge looming shadows rising up along the stone made by those persons crossing the square. It was hardly what I wished to see at the moment, having quite enough to allow my imagination to act as contortionist.

I went back home, sufficiently upset, and found father asleep as I had expected. I stopped briefly in the haunted parlor to drink a glass of kir I had earlier left untouched, and to attempt another playing card collage, this one a fracturing of queens. Then I went upstairs trying to compose myself. As I passed the inhabited room I trembled, trying not to look into it's darkness which appeared vast. I went instead into my small room and sat with my book, and the lights on. It seemed terribly loud on the street, more than it had been any previous night. I was disturbed by this. I looked at the window, but was certain I had latched it earlier that evening and to my eye in the light it appeared closed. Still when I opened and closed the door to the bedroom, preparing for bed, the door would be assisted shut as if an air current were present. I took some brief notes on recent events, something to the effect of 'shadows on cathedral', and 'turned portrait again today, must remember to ask father about this.' 'Doors pushed by hidden wind.' I concluded the brief entry, 'this is all I dare write' having a fear that the presences might be angered at my attempts to record their activities. After I put my journal aside, I did my best to ignore all of this, tried to put unpleasant thoughts out of my head and settled in bed with a letter of Madame Sevigne's beginning "I have still got blotches my dear and I am still taking remedies." However I was soon disturbed by a loud knocking upon what sounded like the front door downstairs. Thinking that it was most likely locked and that if it were father—though I knew him to be asleep—he would certainly try the other entrance, I did not stir, since I was already undressed. But the knocking persisted somewhat more forcefully, and I got out of bed and threw on my robes. This was about midnight. As I was proceeding down the stone steps I heard the knocking again, and a woman's voice very clearly which said 'hallo' in a French accent. I flew to the front door, quite puzzled, and pressed my face to the glass to look out into the darkness. No one was present. I saw only the red roses glowing along the courtyard, which seemed rather bright in the darkness. I went then to the back door. No one was there either. I then very much frustrated went back up stairs to bed, my nerves by now quite dizzy. I tried to read and dozed but did not sleep. I finally did succeed in sleeping then for several hours.

I awoke again in the early hours before dawn. Cords of seaweed about my neck. And blue, we are covered in blue. The tide is blue. The sands are blue. Her expression is blue. My arm around her neck, and her arm around mine. She is carrying me out with her. She is asking me to walk with her.

I try to tell father about the recurring vision. He says, Katherine you must remember the truth. But what truth shall I remember? I saw her walk out into the tidal flats wearing white. I did not see her return.

When I awoke again I was grateful that light was streaming into the room, and the curtains were billowing, at which point I realized that the windows had been open all night, though I was certain that I had both closed and latched them in the early evening.

30 JUILLET 98

I was very good early on in the night. I played music and forgot to worry as I read my book. Now as I write I am so tired I can barely hope to gather the resilience to record the trials of the night, which seem infinite. The day is doubly bright which is a curse on my eyesight, so hooded and retreated I am now. I have given up the thought of sleep entirely after what has occurred. As I said I was lying down with my book, engrossed. At first, I was not bothered by any sounds about the house. For now they there was what seemed a harmless scuffling. I had learned to distinguish father's ambling from any other sounds, and also to determine to some degree from which chamber the sounds had echoed, though the acoustics of the house did take some puzzling over. I had begun to doze with only the little reading light still lit but then sometime around two a.m. the sharper noises began. I knew that father was in bed and the noises also came from several regions of the house at once. I heard some chair scraping, pounding, lots of footsteps, and some shuffling about. I tried in vain to ignore this, since the noises would commence, pause for long enough that

213

I might doze off, and then begin again, rousing me from my semi-conscious state. I kept peering into the darkness and seeing nothing, and hearing either the noises, or the very penetrating quiet in my ears, and wishing that this night would simply come to an end.

Then a shift occurred in the atmosphere; the presences had entered my small room. I perceived a series of minute points of light in a corner of the room and moving towards me. A waft of coldness waving over my body. There are not words to describe what then occurred. A great pressure and thrumming in my body, primarily in my chest. I was shaking uncontrollably. It was as if an electric current were passing through me. I was paralyzed, and could not move even my little finger to try and push the presence away. Since I could think of no other defense, I concentrated all of my thoughts in an effort to rid myself of the intruder. When I did finally succeed, or the presence of it's own desire departed, after what was probably several minutes (though it seemed much longer) I noticed that the room had reverted to it's former state. The atmosphere was clear. I could breathe once again freely, and there were no other disturbances that night. I was too deeply disturbed to sleep after what had occurred. I finally rested some successfully at dawn and then into the late morning and awoke unable to turn my neck—certainly the result of being gripped with fear throughout most of the night.

I walk out along the stone sea wall often in the evenings to watch the sun drop into the sea. This would be about ten o'clock in the summertime. Sometimes the tide is still very low, and I might walk further, beyond the wall, as I did last night, in bare feet. It was a warm evening and the moon was nearly full, a russet color and hanging low. It was one of the lowest tides of the year. The sun had warmed the waters all day, and so as they rose to my ankles and shins I was not bothered. I looked out at the waters which now were like glass. All of the outcroppings of rock were exposed and they seemed to rise higher than they had ever risen before. As the sky softened the lighthouse began to blink, and all of the guiding markers as well, which lead boats through the channel safely.

I stood there for some time. I walked out until the waters brushed my knee, and saw what appeared to be a figure in white, far out on a large rock. This rock, commonly referred to as Roche de Lue, the wolf rock, was one I'd often walked out and climbed up upon when the tides were low. To reach there one would walk through the tidal flats. The vast expanse like some unknown desert, pale sands covered with mounds of circular worm castings, piles of algae in every imaginable hue. The golden brown leaflets resembling tiny evergreen trees, the chartreuse tissue thin triangles, the brilliant pink and red sheathes and fingers of dulse, the brown-green long wavy frills and banners of kelp, the black whistles and tails, and of course the ever long and narrow brackish green tangles of spaghetti of the sea. There would be the occasional crab in a small warm puddle which remained. It was nearly a mile out along the sand flats, among the tide's refuse, out towards the wolf rock, which to reach even at low tides, one had to cross a small channel of water. When the tides were out, the water might reach only to my knees. But the vertical distance between high and low tides was up to forty feet. At high tide only the very top of the rock remained above water. The rock was rutted and chiseled from the waters and appeared as the face of a deeply scared, though not uncharitable guardian of the myriad of forms which perched atop it, or clung beneath its wet caverns. As one grew closer the journey became precarious, since even though the tide might be low, there was so much algae that it was impossible to see the many rocks along the way. Sludging through the thick bottom proved hazardous. Not only was it covered in slippery algae, but the spaghetti seaweed was so dense and swirled by the tides that it also had the potential to trip you, or tie you where you were. When finally I reached the rock, I would climb up along one of it's lower caverns and sit on a bed of very soft and pleasant sea-weed. My eyes were at once drawn to the underside of the rock, onto which clung thousands of tiny red ascidi-ans, flecked with some green and yellow. It appeared somewhat like the giant and fleshy mouth of the giant stone, or some undiscovered soft tissue of stalactites. I bent my head underneath the rock and then also heard the sound of the barnacles, opening and closing, spewing water. It was near to impossible to look beneath the rock without getting seawater into ones eyes or mouth, so busy were it's inhabitants filtering.

This was hardly the hour for a journey to the wolf rock. I looked at the figure again. The tide was about her waist. I walked out towards her, very carefully as not to lose my footing on the seaweed covered rocks. I looked back and saw the seawall was completely covered. It took me some time to come near to her. By this time the tide was to her chest, close to her throat, tossing her hair about in the wind. And I had not noticed this but the water must have been to my waist. I felt oddly warm. I followed the figure every time I looked up, though it was difficult to see through the waters, which were swelling about me, and of course I could see nothing below my knees since the water was rushing. I looked up again just in time to see the figure vanish. I felt a wave of remorse, and noticed that I had been shivering. Then I looked about me hardly trusting my vision as to what I had seen, and immediately realizing my dilemma. The waters would soon be over my head, and the rocks hidden. I turned hastily back. If it had not been a bright moon who knows how I would have managed. It took me quite some time and as I slowly lifted each ankle and felt with hands and knees for the next lunge forward I determined that the figure might have been no more than moonlight. An odd spill against a rock. She vanished as easily as she had appeared. By the time I had reached the stone wall I was drenched to the roots of my hair and was very relieved to find Alain out walking on the other side of the wall over the tall rocks. I must have appeared as an apparition, since when he saw me he nearly lost his footing and fell himself, so shocked was he to see me emerging from the tides. He called my name uncertainly. I nodded, beginning to shiver again as I was now mostly out of the water, and exposed more fully to the night air. He took off his coat, wrapped it around me, and walked along in the dark with me to the chateau, all the while scolding me in French for my reckless behavior. I said nothing to him about what I had seen, nor of course to father, not wishing to worry him. Though he looked at me with more disappointment than concern, once he knew that I was all right.

But what has come of this episode, besides spoiling Alain's coat and worrying my family? I now give up my hesitations to water. I remain on dry land. She can no longer linger about me. Moonlight upon stone. My shoulders will not bear her touch. And though I have promised myself this many times before, I pledge now to give her back her own phrases of water, her palace of the unseen, and not to walk into the ocean at night.

I thought that all of the portraits were mine. But these hands will no longer speak truthfully. And this is why I can convince them of nothing.

iii

THE BOWER

"Bower is a secluded place where they had names. Find their names"
— Gertrude Stein

THE BOWER

There is nowhere to begin within a bower which contains naught. There they met and there the red-winged sparrow insisted upon gathering pearl-seed. But the pearls are light, replied the lily-of-the-lawn, and the seed is naught. The lily with soft manicured petals and hands of gracious loveliness. The lily was spotted with light and dampness and therefore full with light. The sparrow asked the difference between nowhere and a bower. The lily replied stringing the light into a necklace. If you say seed, you imply thought. And the sparrow marked the generous eyes of the lily and saw that her pale hands could be for herself like a soft sitting room.

They were drinking the tea of a reddish root. The sky had befallen white numbness. Blankets overcame them to dross. A bower bird constructs a bower to attract a lover, and is known to steal fetching tokens, such as pale mosses and silken ribbon. The sparrow was not such a bird, but a bird in a bower imagined. Not a bird constructing. To sleep, replied the sparrow silently, and the lily pleated her garments and made a place for her, knowing that though she was not tired the descent to sleep is tiered as the deepest set gown. The sky might become tundra. She twisted her tongue and said nothing of accomplishments, or the tint of the shortening day. Summer was an inkling. The dyed grasses changed their hemispheres and shrank as the sense of the sparrow's cumbersome tasks. To be set to gathering seed.

The lily sighed. A word is a sigh and so is a silence. Pearl does not come of seed, she said, but of sequestering. A bower is that tundra, that terrace or furnace or lawn where one may construct a series of preoccupations, and study them, internally. Repeat the names of those calming vestibules. The names they had found might have suited an orchestra, a tapestry, a beach scene. Nevertheless the glade had become a bower. A bower is a secluded place where a lily becomes a sitting room. Where light becomes pearl. Mother of nacreous fields. To thee in this bower a sparrow becomes a question. Did they find their names? Or had their names located them beforehand?

The question is of possession, that which is a found name possesses what may be found in a bower. One may have little—but one must have a bower of self-possession.

Her secret could no longer be kept. He knew already, as they walked along the shore at dusk. Already she was pensive and he followed the path of the moon. The tide was very low. One horizon red, the other blue which edged into smoke, and the dark rocks becoming darker still, gleaming wet. She'd come to tell him about the letters, about Marion, about Katherine, and all of this given over in a clipped fashion. He barely had time to readjust his understanding because she was rushing along in order to reach the most recent outcropping.

He was alarmed at how much had changed in such a short time. He begged her to slow her telling. It all seemed implausible. Unlikely as she hurried along, skirts tossing about, arms gesturing in a similar manner.

"Don't you see?" she said, ignoring his plea that she retreat and recover the quick steps she had taken, "More so than I ever imagined they might be—my questions have been answered."

"How is that?" he asked, still more puzzled.

"She wished for me to find all of this out," she spoke to the distances ahead of her. "What I don't understand," she continued, "is why Katherine has agreed. But then perhaps she has not. Not knowing her—how could I tell?"

He was wondering, how could she tell what?

But she seemed not to notice his uncertain look. "There is something odd about her mother. About the disappearance. About her being abroad. It is uncertain."

She stopped for a moment for which he was grateful. But then she went on again at the same pace. "The only thing I have determined is the reason I have been left with this portfolio." She eyed him now to see if he had guessed.

He had not. His endless questions carried them further, beyond the wet rocks, and the blue sky which had now become violet, and past the small harbor, masts standing stark like the skeletons of trees. "Katherine?" he asked, "agreed to what? Are you certain of what you saw in the house? Are you certain that those works were Clara's?"

She answered, as she could, minutely, according to the details which struck her, but as they walked her mind ran on along different ledges. It seemed so small to her, what she might accomplish.

VIOLETTE FEVER

I am the cause of her fever, (her flight, she thought) and I will not leave her side until she is well. Kiss the left ear three times saying To thee!—For thee!—With thee! Amelia desired to set aside this volume of tales which drew her to cutting wood in a forest, clinging tightly to a trembling tree. She wished to arrange her bed of mosses, to allow sleep to possess her senses. But once again the hideous toad crept upon her shutter.

There could be no more question about identity. No more cities disappearing into waves. Was that what Clara had meant that day in the gallery when she had asked her to be a subject herself? Herself displaced firmly along landscapes. Borrowed, placed here against a bronze sea, a foot of silver and a hand of gold. An eye to mark a signature, a false signature. The scrawl of a toad? She was not mere vapor, a monogram, a faulty mirror. None of this had been imagined. She had come near to doubting she had ever embraced such a creature. To find that she had a history. But actuality did not quell fever. Staunch dreams and burrowed desire.

She went over and over again her last meeting with Marion. Her room, this bower correctly obliging her. Her mother, who ought to know. I am her other and I ought to know. I am her reflection and I ought to dislike you. I am one interior upon which you have treaded. I'm sorry Marion, she said towards the missing toad. You are not that, though you do creep along my shutter. I am the one who has crept. You who are not Katherine. I am not Katherine. Katherine is nowhere. The question remained, where was Clara? But for the first time in what seemed to her centuries of some vast wintry hemisphere, the question did not burrow. The question did not beg her. Instead another question etched itself into what seemed her marrow. That which will quell this fever, she thought is no longer pondering who will be I and who will be she. I am within the borders of my own quenched skin. The room stands upright. I do miss her, the changeling of this sumptuous bower once shared. But utterly I understand the evidence. She wished me to act.

Why does a ghost appear? Something amiss. She gives me an object in question not located upon her death. She carried this portfolio to save her sister from becoming her reflection. In the process I have become her sister. My peril was once her peril. But I am no longer reflection. I was as she was. But now my skin carries weight. My voice inflection. Then from this forward road onward, the toad may have no word with me. I may remove my reflection from her mirror. That is the secret to unlocking the mysterious lives of objects. They must compass a living being. And once discovering the reason given, a token may be returned.

The Shards and the Mirror

He walked out into the day as if it were not merely bright, and with a particular errand. With the deft and graceful movements which accompanied his every endeavor. He walked interacting with the ground beneath him.

Perhaps he will save another from a vision slipped, such double vision which may mistake the neighborhood entirely. Too few accomplishments is not the same as too many accidents. Too many spectators is not the same as too many speculations. Too many spectacles ruin the view.

He walked away from that destination she had been courting. It fell beneath her more mildly than he might have expected. And she surrendered it with the self assurance of stepping away from her own reflection. She took one long look, and then gave away what had been given. Like all things received it could not be kept.

He walked up the stone steps. He asked directions, though he knew where he was going. And though he had been here on many occasions, he looked about him as if he had not. He approached the information desk and placed the black portfolio on the counter. There was an envelope attached, and a name.

LETTER TO CLARA

I have disbelieved history

and found a hidden facet

I've returned the indelible impression

one sister for another

stepped out of this gilt frame

I give away this portrait

passage below the rose

your dress of shadows

which once walked itself

Levitate: to rise in defiance to gravity. To float. Against the laws of nature. To hover. Opposed to gravitate, or gravity. With reference to spiritualism. In virtue of lightness. A woman levitated to the ceiling, floated, and glided out the window into the garden. To make less weight. The scientific—to cause something denser than fluid surrounding to suspend using magnetic forces. The field is anti-gravitational, akin to the dormitive quality of opium.

Birds have atmospheric and levitational information which millions of years will not render accessible to us. Apium graveolens, seeds of celery eaten before flight to avoid dizziness. Brassica, seed of mustard, used to travel through air. Populus tremuloides, Poplar, added to flying ointments and placed upon the body.

AMELIA'S DREAM OF THE SPARROW AND THE TOAD

But how did she get on when the other did not return? She laid down the question, which she had carried until fatigued, as if within an iron cloak. She drew aside the days, this sparrow of days and alighted upon a day beyond winter. Must the spring light penetrate everywhere, she asked?

No, answered the toad. But she did not listen. The spring light blotted out the toad. You are not even a toad she said. Not as comely, nor as promising. A toad represents all things which should be loved but which may be overlooked. I have not overlooked you. I have grown tired of studying you. You dwell in the river seen with eyes closed. And if I drown the image I will not be returned to myself. There is no drowning such an image. Such a token must be returned.

Pertaining To Twilight

The tracks are barely dim enough and every waiting space is taken. A wash of red color suffuses the tunnel and remains for approximately three minutes during which time the train approaches. First a dim gleam, and then clouds of vapor, bright light, metal upon metal. Amelia confuses the scene—an earlier dream, a heady recollection, blinding her senses. This time the train is completely empty. She returns dramatically to the present. Clearly, there is nothing to be told. No one within the train before her. Place in front of her a mirror and she will not believe what she now sees.

The tracks are covered with the light from the train and every seat will soon be taken as the crowds prod and crowd around the entrance. Amelia straightens her edges and walks down the aisle towards the front of the train, sits beside a wide window, and looks out at the rest of the crowd in the station, still moving towards the entrance.

The train is barely dim and her profile is pressed against the glass, casting an angular shadow on the seat across from her. She is very tired. Imagines lying down on her back. Her dress is tangled around her legs and her hair spills over her chin, obscuring her expression. She folds her arms, and closes her eyes.

The train is barely dim and the boarding increment has nearly ended, the red lights blink signaling departure, and then in her seat she contemplates for half of one thought only, whether or not to proceed. The half thought passes quickly, and the train has exited the station through the tunnel, not willing to discuss what no conscious deliberation has caused. Most likely she did not wish to learn the reason for her travel, and she was tired, too very tired to be cross-examined by the conductor, and so continued on her way, to lapse in and out of sleep, somewhat carelessly.

Looking out the window, fog moving in thickets, appearing and disappearing. Her memory a luxurious pendulum which swings.

If I were to board a train and you were to board a train—.

She recalls, speed has no image, a ray of disentangled seeing. She is still entangled with magnificent words which no one uses.

If I were to board this disbelief, I would travel at the same rate as the average afternoon. But the afternoon has contained lengthy shadows. The thousand and one eyes along the surface of the waters.

The interminable winter pauses. The ground softens. The train has come apart.

There are artists who carry light and those who carry sound, and those with capital letters only.

She stops off near the water. She finds a stick and digs a hole in the ground near lily of the lawn. A red-winged blackbird lands upon a pendulum. Along the surface of the water, she catches her reflection pulling the letter from her coat pocket, placing it into the ground, covering it. Brushstrokes away from the shore.

She sits upon a picnic table, shoulders sloped. Imagines a voice in the distance. A child is running towards the water.

LAYNIE BROWNE is the author of several books, including *Gravitys Mirror*, *The Agency of Wind*, *Lore* and *Rebecca Letters*. With others, she has curated poetry series at The Ear Inn in New York City from 1992-1995, and later as a member of The Subtext Collective in Seattle 1996-2001. She was awarded The Gertrude Stein Award in Innovative American Poetry three times (1993-1996). In 1998 her work was anthologized in the book Poet's Choice, edited by former poet laureate Robert Hass. In 2000, she received a Jack Straw Writers Program Award. She has taught poetry-in-the-schools in New York City and Seattle. Currently she resides in Oakland, California.

,

Printed in Great Britain
by Amazon